THE LONGEST NIGHT

Also by Otto de Kat in English translation

OTTO DE KAT

THE LONGEST NIGHT

Translated from the Dutch
by Laura Watkinson

MacLehose Press
New York • London

MacLehose Press
An imprint of Quercus
New York • London

© 2017 by Otto de Kat
English Translation © 2017 by Laura Watkinson
First published in the United States by Quercus in 2017

ISBN 978-1-68144-199-3

Library of Congress Control Number: 2017901504

Distributed in the United States and Canada by
Hachette Book Group
1290 Avenue of the Americas
New York, NY 10104

This book is a work of fiction. Names, characters, institutions, places, and events are either the product of the author's imagination or are used fictitiously. Any resemblance to actual persons—living or dead—events, or locales is entirely coincidental.

Manufactured in the United States

10 9 8 7 6 5 4 3 2 1

www.quercus.com

For Verena and Clarita, daughters of Adam and Clarita von Trott,
and in memory of Christabel Bielenberg

1

"What day is it, nurse?"

"It's Sunday."

"He's coming on Tuesday."

The nurse nodded, she had heard, he would be arriving from Germany in the morning. And the doctor would be coming in the afternoon, and then the team.

"What time is it, nurse?"

"Nine o'clock."

"In the morning or the evening?"

"In the evening. Look, it's almost dark."

Emma knew exactly what day it was, and what time, and what was going to happen. Her questions were a smoke screen, she wanted the nurse to think she was already quite far gone.

"Mother, do you still recall how we, as the day grew long, sat by the window when I was small, and every night we'd sing a song?" Emma softly spoke the lines to herself. The windows were open, it was still warm. A huge moon hung above the row of houses in the distance. Some of them had lights on inside. From Oudedijk came the sounds of bells ringing and trams and cars and the high, plaintive wail of mopeds.

"Tired from jumping, tired from fun, on your lap in the fading light, ready for bed, your little son, I'd think of the mysteries of the night." Emma turned and saw that the woman who would soon help her to bed was listening with surprise.

"Someone wrote those words a very long time ago, nurse, I think even before I was born, that poet has been with me a long while. There are so many of his lines that I've never been able to forget."

The nurse pulled up the blanket that had slipped from Emma's lap. "Aren't you cold?"

Reciting the poem from memory—that was rather impressive.

"As we sang that song without a name, a song with words so tried and true, an age-old song, and ever the same, about God who watches all we do . . ." She hesitated. "Never without shaking, Mother, could you sing that old refrain."

She had forgotten a couple of lines, nothing rhymed with "refrain." She searched, but could not find the rhyme. But that did not matter, as the most important and saddest part had been said: that they sang about how God watches all we do.

Did He really? That wasn't the impression she had. Her God, the God she had believed in so strongly and so sincerely, defending Him, even against her own better judgment, seeking Him and praising Him, but now finding Him nowhere. And yet those lines of poetry filled her with an all-encompassing emotion. She did not understand how a few rhyming words could take hold of her and awaken an ancient longing. That age-old song, ever the same. She had once sung it, had heard its music. The notes had vanished now though, there was no song, only the sounds of the evening on Oudedijk. That song. But which song was it? Her life had shattered into fragments, crystal clear, light and dark, an endless flow. Time turned upside down, and inside out.

"No, I'm not cold. Not yet."

Emma smiled cautiously. Before she could say anything else, the jangling din of the nurse's mobile telephone rang out.

2

They are among the few who still have a connection, and now the telephone will not stop ringing. An aggressive caller. Or a frightened one?

Emma watches the telephone, scarcely able to bear the sound. Is it Carl, is it the Ministry, is it the Gestapo, about to arrest them? No, they don't call, they just march right into your house. She does not dare to answer, holds herself back even as she becomes convinced it must be Carl.

"Never answer the telephone, Emma," he had impressed upon her. "We're not in. Only if I call with our code."

The day she ignores that telephone, it is July 25. Ignoring as much as possible will maybe give them a chance of getting through it, she tells herself.

Since the 20th, the days had been short and the nights long, and Emma and Carl had lived in a pressure cooker of fear and tension. Every footstep outside, every creaking floorboard, every passing stranger, every car on the street, every door that opens. They say that fear paralyses, and it's true. The brain no longer works as it should, it's as if some substance is released that swamps ordinary reactions. Nothing adheres to the rules of normality anymore.

The bomb under the conference table in Hitler's headquarters had killed people, but the wrong ones. The divine leader himself had escaped and had welcomed his Italian friend Mussolini that same afternoon, the smoke still around his head, battered and bruised—the photographers had recorded it a thousand times. The event had placed a bomb under Carl and Emma's lives too, hundreds of kilometers away, on the wrong side of the table.

And yet Carl still went to his job at the Ministry of Foreign Affairs, just as he had for four years. The neighbors in Berlin-Dahlem would have seen him walking to the U-Bahn station as usual, if they had been paying attention.

Adam von Trott, Carl's boss, had called a meeting. The agenda looked harmless, packed with routine business. For days and nights they had discussed whether he should obey Adam's summons. Carl had flatly repeated, and repeated, that he could not say no, Emma knew she could not stop him. Carl, her husband, whom she loves better than anyone, and yet she has to let him go because he cannot abandon von Trott. Not at this moment, not at this turning point. Solidarity versus love, betrayal versus future. Friendship versus flight. His life or his wife. The nights had passed in conflict and in silence.

Now morning is stealing into their garden with the chirping of the birds, it is the height of summer, a day is being carved from the darkness. They do not know if they will see each other again this evening. Carl attempts a few words, Emma just looks at him. Their embrace is almost fleeting, three, four seconds, she feels his arm around her, his hand brush her cheek. She does not cry.

They have agreed that she must have a suitcase ready so she can leave the house at a moment's notice. In the event

of an emergency she intends to seek refuge with Mr. Wapenaar, a friend of her father's, who lives in Grunewald, fifteen
minutes away by bicycle. In the event of an emergency: their
entire existence has become an emergency. Carl and she
have clung to the promise of a rapidly approaching end to
the war. An end that has shifted, year in, year out. Everyone
is speculating, everyone is sure, this cannot go on much longer. Until finally no one believes it anymore, even von Trott
had said he did not know what would happen. Von Trott!
Their friend, whom they blindly trust and follow, no matter
where he goes.

In the middle of the war Carl and Adam had traveled to
Sweden, Switzerland and Portugal, neutral countries with
indifferent people who viewed them as traitors. Under the
pretense of carrying out useful diplomatic missions for Germany, they had made cautious contact with the Allies. They
told them about the growing resistance against Hitler, about
the antipathy of the generals, they asked for support for the
moment when the leader would finally be eliminated. But it
was no good. No one trusted them. Resistance against Hitler,
big deal. Desertion, that was what it was. They were oppor-
tunists, changing course just in time, cowards full of noble
words. They had been miserable journeys through a crum-
bling Europe.

Carl and Emma's isolation has increased over the years. In
Dahlem, their suburb of Berlin, where the violence penetrates
only rarely, a person could occasionally believe none of it is
true, that it is peace as usual. In the heat of July, for instance,
when the gardens are quiet, when there is no traffic, no soldiers,
and no falling bombs. But now, in the days following the assassination attempt, the reign of terror has once again erupted in
full force.

That damned telephone, ringing all morning as she stood staring at it, and then following her throughout the house and into the garden, where there is no escape. It is not the code we agreed, I am not going to answer, we are not in, you can call until the cows come home.

Carl left at seven this morning, as usual. Past the garden hedge and into the street, it takes ten minutes to reach the station, he was at the office at eight o'clock sharp, the meeting was due to begin at nine. At ten they started calling, ten, twenty, thirty times. Why? She is wrong, it *must* be Carl.

She picks up the telephone and does not speak, waits, for a threat or reassurance, stands with the receiver in her hand, ready for the guillotine.

"Frau Regendorf, it's me, Ulla. Thank goodness I've got hold of you! They've taken your husband, and everyone else in the meeting, they took Herr von Trott and your husband to Prinz-Albrecht-Strasse. You need to leave right now, your husband said they'll come for the families too."

The ax has fallen. The killer has invaded her house in the guise of a loyal secretary. Ulla, the executioner.

Emma stammers something, hangs up, then tries to call back to thank Ulla, but the line is busy. Her suitcase is packed and waiting, some clothes, photographs, papers, a marriage reduced to a box with a handle on it, easy enough to carry, yet so hard to bear. She looks around. The room with its view of the garden is silent, tranquil. Dining table, bookshelves, the house is full and motionless, and terrifyingly empty.

Luckily her bicycle still works. She puts the case on the luggage rack and holds it in place behind her with one hand, for as long as it takes. Exactly a quarter of an hour. She pedals onward mechanically, along the idyllic lanes of leafy Grunewald, guilty neighborhood of wealth and collaboration. Adriaan Wapenaar must be an exception, as he is by no means wealthy or obliging. Married to Elka, a German, he works as a Dutchman under a Swedish flag. This has made him a point of refuge for the hundreds of his compatriots flowing through Berlin or stranded there, on their way to nowhere, fleeing, escaping labor in the factories somewhere outside the city.

She has to get inside without being seen, in case Wapenaar's house is being watched. At every bend in the road she expects a checkpoint, behind every tree a soldier. But no one appears, the streets remain deathly quiet.

The gate is open, she rides down the short driveway, which is lined with rosebushes, she recognizes it all from the last time she visited, three years ago.

"Emma!"

Wapenaar calls from the garden and runs over to her. "Careful, Emma. I'll help you, give me your suitcase."

He is followed by Elka. They take her round to the side of the house, where no one can see her from the road, then they shut the conservatory doors and sit her down in a chair.

Wapenaar does not ask her anything, he already understands. He knows that open season has been declared on the families and acquaintances of those who conspired against the "Divine One." Even friends of friends of friends are suspect, a name in a diary, a meeting years ago, a telephone conversation, everything is being investigated. The neighbor, the maid, the children's teacher, all of them are under suspicion, all of them could end up on a list for interrogation, all of them will have their opportunity to testify and to vilify. Wapenaar knows the methods that the scum employ, and he channels his fear into effective sabotage.

It is a crucial hour, there around the table with the Wapenaars, slowly working out what to do, where to go, how to stay out of the hands of the hunters. They decide that Emma will have a room upstairs until they find out where Carl is, and what is going to happen to him. Wapenaar says that she can always stay with relatives of Elka's in the Black Forest, in a Nazi-free village. They still exist, villages of people who are concerned mainly about their cows and more or less ignore the war.

3

"Would you like me to take you back to bed?"

Emma looked up. The dark rooms around her already felt strange. Her patiently collected objects and heirlooms were scattered about the room, with no gleam to them, seemingly at random, she had not touched them for ages, no longer looked at them, all the things that had ever held meaning for her seemed stiff and soulless. Things were like people, she had always thought, except a lot easier to keep with you.

"Of how His marvels and His making preserve us time and time again . . ."

"What's that?"

"Again, refrain, the line that rhymes with refrain, I'd forgotten it, but it's come back to me now."

Emma saw the nurse's doubt, her brief confusion about what to think of the woman beside her, who spoke in riddles and yet was so lucid. Who seemed as close as she was far away.

She showed no intention of going to bed. The warm evening air blew in through the window, to all appearances she was safe here, there was no threat that she had not brought upon herself. She barely noticed the nurse going to the kitchen. There were only the echoes of an old life, her years in Leeuwarden, Berlin, the Black Forest, the street where she had now lived for more than sixty years. That street was a block of basalt in a river, worn and weathered, with Emma and her concrete memory up above, on the third floor.

The street. When exactly was it that she first came to the flat she would never leave? The war had gone underground, it was 1946, there were babies popping out all over, and in the city a crane every hundred meters. The motto was: Make babies and buildings. "Liberated and impregnated"—that was what the women were. And that also meant being bound hand and foot. Emma had seen the children in their street growing up, playing marbles and football with their fathers, endlessly skipping and hiding and seeking. In the early summer evenings, an ice-cream van drove down the street, and in the winter the coalman carried his sacks to the cellars, and every day the baker climbed the stairs with his basket. Dressed in their pajamas, the children would go across the road to someone's father, who would do gymnastic exercises with them, or to a neighbor who would read Nils Holgersson's adventures to them. The 1950s, a world that had long ago been torn to shreds.

Emma had emerged from the woods of the Black Forest like a ghost, without Carl, parched with grief.

The journey to the Netherlands had been worse than the bombings she had endured in Berlin. It was chaos, gangs were pillaging the countryside, and there was a constant threat of rape or murder: the Middle Ages, the Thirty Years' War, the peace of '45.

A woman traveling alone was a provocation. Emma had cut her hair short. With a cap on, she looked from a distance like a man. A handsome man, though, and handsome men were in just as much danger.

First she went to Switzerland, in search of her father, but the Swiss had turned her away at the border, as her father had left the country months before. She was German too, and the Swiss were suddenly not so keen on their northern neighbors.

The trek that followed took three weeks, from Basel back into Germany, via Freiburg, Karlsruhe, Trier, on a bus, in a truck bulging with people, in a Jeep with soldiers, part of the way on a freight train, and walking, endlessly walking across a scorched landscape. Emma forged a route up through Germany, she had to get out of Germany, and eventually reached Aachen, a sea of senseless ruins.

She arrived at the Dutch border in one piece, and her father's name finally lifted her up and over: Verschuur, Foreign Affairs, Resistance. After lengthy negotiation she was allowed to continue on her way. But where to? Her mother lived in London, having moved there just before the invasion. Going to London was not an option. Besides, Emma was not inclined to try to find her, even before the war she rarely saw her. She did not know where her father was.

With an ice-cold heart, she entered Limburg, a province that was even less Dutch than the country where she had lived with Carl. Carl. Even the thought of him could not warm her, she felt nothing now, she was chilled through. But her will not to go under was stronger than her desire to jump in front of a train. No matter how cold and frozen, she would live, as long as she could, against the odds, on top of the ruins.

After a day surrounded by that incomprehensible dialect, she had decided to head for Rotterdam, to Gouda, where the factory belonging to her mother's family, the Dudoks, should be. Before the war they had shipped machines all over the world, but it would not surprise her to find the factory destroyed, bankrupt. She remembered a nice cousin. Maybe he still lived there. She had barely known her Dutch family. Her father's parents had died young, and her grandmother on her mother's side, a woman she had come to love more than she did her own mother, had not survived the war.

Emma had no idea who or what she would find in Holland.

4

"Bruno Verweij."

For a moment the name hangs in the air. She listens, hears how modestly he pronounces it, or no, casually more like, as if his name does not matter, as if he is interested only in hers. Emma is standing in a small circle of people who are chatting away. The man, who is called Bruno Verweij, is not at its center, but Emma instantly senses that the group would lose its cohesion without him. He is nothing at all like Carl, and yet there is a vague resemblance.

"Emma Regendorf," she says, with a German "g." She has his complete attention.

The spring of 1946 is cold. Deep into March there are still remnants of snow lying in places the sun cannot reach. Other sources of warmth have to be found.

Emma has been taken to this club, De Reünie, by her cousin Chris Dudok and his wife Imke, with whom she is staying until she finds a house and a job.

It has been six months since she arrived on their doorstep with a suitcase in her hand and a cap on her head. A statue and a caricature.

Chris had answered the door. His welcome was strange and confusing. He had turned deathly pale, and it seemed as if he had been waiting for her, as if he wanted to take her in his arms.

"Do you recognize me, Chris? It's me, Emma, Emma Verschuur."

"Christ, Emma! For a moment I thought . . ." He took a step back as if to rewind, to undo his actions of a moment before.

Emma was welcomed like a long-lost daughter. She could stay as long as she wanted, there was plenty of room, no, really, she couldn't be more welcome, Chris said happily. She was given two rooms with a view of the canal beside the house and, diagonally opposite, the large entrance doors to Chris' factory, Dudok's Machine Works. She had stepped into a book of fairy tales, a hazy negative of a pre-war photograph, but the real world was gone, nothing in any way resembled what she had seen in all those years of war. Standing at her window, looking and listening to the water, the passers-by, sometimes a barge that docked at the factory, the sounds of metal on metal drifting across during loading and unloading, nothing really reached her.

It is nice and busy at De Reünie. Groups cluster around the billiards table, new people keep arriving, bringing a blast of cold with them. There is a feeling that they have plenty to celebrate. Post-war reconstruction in a provincial town, so full of expectations, so almost naïve. Their little club has survived those foul years after all. The Krauts are gone for good, thank God. Prosperity is not yet here, but the band is playing this evening, like old times, the first songs of longing fill the parlor once again, the bridge tables are occupied, the cards are shuffled. Saturday night is the regular music night, and sometimes there's dancing too. Just because, for no real reason, a respectable kind of mischief.

"Where do you live, Mr. Verweij?"

"Would you please call me Bruno? And may I call you Emma?"

She nods. His question is as simple as it is friendly. In Germany, where the path to familiarity can be endless, that question would have taken far longer to come.

"In Rotterdam, in a street where the war was only a rumor. And you?"

"More or less around the corner, Regentesseplantsoen, on Kattensingel, at Chris Dudok's."

"I know Chris very well, we grew up not far from each other, my father used to be mayor here, I'm afraid. But as for me, I feel more comfortable in Rotterdam than anywhere else. Six years in that city, in a perfectly ordinary street, and you're sold. Well, I'm speaking for myself, of course—you might run a mile."

He's not saying anything special, but what she hears sounds strangely familiar. There is an intimacy she has not experienced for a long time. For almost two years she has been living in a daze, her body has become a strange object in which she has barely any interest. But right now she can feel how Bruno is looking at her, as only a man can. Now and then. Without intent, as a kind of greeting, with a certain awe of the unfathomable.

The music begins. He bows. Does she want to dance? She hasn't danced since her birthday party, in the blacked-out past of Berlin. June 1941, she still remembers it in detail and yet she wants to forget. She returns his bow, places one hand on his arm, and he leads her to the dance floor, which extends between the tightly packed tables and chairs like a hole in the ice. Their feet slide incredulously across the parquet. She has not been this close to a man for years.

"*Ich bin von Kopf bis Fuss*"—are they really playing that song? Just like before, when Carl whirled her round and round, the windows covered with black paper, the gramophone with its big horn high up on a bookcase, the voice of Marlene Dietrich in a room full of friends. The warning sounded, the adrenaline raced as they listened to that forbidden song by that forbidden singer. No song had ever sounded like this in the land of the enemy, in the land of her husband.

Here, at De Reünie at least, everything is friendly and civilized. Emma feels no threat, the windows are open to allow in a little fresh air. Then she and Bruno dance past an enormous mirror and Emma sees herself. She is moving, apparently dancing, holding someone she does not know, and she herself is someone who is being held. As if she has come home, found herself, there in the mirror. Bruno seems to notice her bewilderment and stops dancing.

"Shall I take you back to Chris now, or would you like something to drink?"

Why do his innocent sentences affect her, even move her, so much?

"Yes, please, I haven't danced for a long time. This calls for a glass of wine. Red."

Bruno puts his arm around her waist to guide her through the throng. Carefully, without any suggestion of insistence. She glances sideways at him, and sees that his ear is wrapped in a thin gauze bandage. She had not noticed it before, but finds it disarming. The imperfection of his face does not put her off at all, on the contrary.

They stay at the club until late. It is one of those evenings that imperceptibly turns into night and then almost touches morning. Emma is asked to dance a few more times by her cousin's friends. Chris will not set foot on the dance floor for anything, he watches the group from the sidelines. And Emma keeps trying to find her way back to Bruno. She feels that her behavior is irrational, they do not know each other, she does not even want to attract his attention, solitary as she has become.

Bruno asks her one more time. When the bandleader announces the last dance, everyone chooses a partner, even Chris ventures onto the dance floor with Imke. Bruno, the announcement taking him by surprise, is just in time to steal Emma away from the advances of a rather tipsy man. She sees him making his way across the floor toward her at a surprising speed, acts as if she has not been watching him and says she would be happy to dance again. But they do little dancing. A forest of elbows and shoes and constant little collisions forces them almost to a standstill. Their hands fixed, his on her hip, hers on his shoulder, in slow motion. Laughter and chatter around them, stumbling and apologies on all sides, the music can scarcely be heard above it all, they do not know how late it is, how tired the heart. For one brief moment, their heads touch. She feels her ear brush against his bandaged ear, and a sensation from a long time ago stirs within her.

Emma is back in Holland.

5

Now it really was getting cold. The nurse had already come a few times to ask if she needed help, but Emma had just shaken her head. She wanted to sit there a while longer, listening to the night and to Oudedijk slowly falling silent. Her carer had once confessed that she thought it amusing and a little old-fashioned to be addressed as "nurse," you could picture the starched caps and aprons. But there was also something soothing about "nurse," a word that warded off doom. Was that what was approaching? Her doom?

"When exactly did I have my fall, nurse?"

"It was four months ago now. In the kitchen."

"And how long have you been here, Judith?"—sometimes she called her Judith instead of "nurse."

"Almost three months."

"I feel like a stranger everywhere, except for in eternity."

"What did you say?"

"Vroman, it was Vroman who wrote that, Leo Vroman, a poet. As if he knew how I feel, everything about that line is exactly right."

It had been a bad fall. She had fetched the stepladder and had struggled up it to get a tin from a high cupboard, a tin she did not really need. It was foolish. A woman of ninety-six should not be climbing ladders and risking her neck. Of course Emma had come a cropper. The stepladder had slipped and the crash had brought a neighbor rushing upstairs. She found Emma on the kitchen floor, bent double with pain. A bone was sticking out from her wrist at an angle.

She went from hospital—"we're going to have to splint it, my love"—to the rehabilitation center and, from there, back home. It was all a matter of slowly disappearing. About four months it took, and then off came the splint and the sling, her feet were useless, and her soul was transformed. Demons appeared from every nook and cranny. Emma was rehabilitated until finally she vanished.

Judith pushed Emma through to the bedroom, in a narrow wheelchair, through a home from which all the obstacles had been removed.

"To bed, to bed, said Sleepyhead, tarry a while, said Slow. Put on the pan, said Greedy Nan. Let's sup before we go!"

Emma laughed. The nurse looked at her, dumbfounded.

"Are you hungry?"

"I certainly am, nurse. Aren't you?"

"But you're not going to eat anything, you discussed this with the doctor, you were going to stop eating, remember?"

"I remember everything, Judith. And that agreement still stands, but I'm ignoring it, just for now. Would you bring me a cracker with jam? I'm sure it won't kill me."

It sounded funny and that was how she had intended it. A cracker with jam, a small nod to eternity.

A little reluctantly, Judith brought her a cracker with jam and three raspberries on it, Emma's favorite fruit. She had bushes full of them in her garden in Dahlem, the memory had not gone, a stubborn image that had persisted throughout the years. Her raspberry bushes, they were probably still there. How old did those bushes get, as old as people? As old as a tortoise or an elephant? Mysterious fruits, you had to pick them with respect or the blood would soon drip all over your fingers. She had made them into jam, boiled them and bottled them, she had a cellar full of mismatched pots and jars.

Carl used to love it.

6

"Adam can walk into the trap without you, you know. You don't really have to go to that meeting, you do realize just how dangerous it is, don't you?"

One last time, she tries to convince Carl. But it is a rear-guard action, a brief skirmish between hope and fear. Emma actually agrees with Carl, he can't abandon Adam, his friend in good times and bad. One for all, all for one—all for nothing? Adam is married too, he and his wife have two children.

The night of July 24 was the most difficult one. It is a night that looms up later, at unguarded and unwanted moments, a night in which Emma becomes lost.

"What's going to happen to our children now?"

Emma and Carl are lying naked, next to each other, on their backs, eyes open, hand in hand, it is four o'clock, just before the first birds wake. Carl turns to her and repeats her words, confused. "Our children?"

"I mean that they'll never exist."

"So you don't think I was doing my best just now?"

He snorts with laughter, and so does Emma, in spite of the leaden weight of her words.

They will never exist, it is a threat of the worst kind, a vision of the end. A last-ditch attempt to change fate? Something like that, yes.

Emma's sense of abandonment is bigger than the bed they are lying in, bigger than their house, it extends over the year when she lived with Carl and back into her childhood, to the days when her parents left her with her grandparents, all on her own. Carl beside her, Carl on top of her, inside her, Carl who loves her but is unable to protect her from these times of destruction and persecution. Who will soon go to Adam's meeting, there is no escaping it.

As a last resort, she asks if that means he does not want to become a father. It is almost an indecent proposal, it sounds like disapproval, and she knows he cannot answer. But why doesn't he say anything at all, why doesn't he say anything else after his little joke, why doesn't he give a sign, a sigh, even tears if need be, or a protest, or a question for her, just something, anything?

A weighty silence hangs in the air, echoing dread, judgment will come soon. It is a night that is not a night, but an exercise in waiting.

She looks at Carl's silhouette, dark against a blacked-out window, impossible for the enemy to find, in that remote corner of Berlin. Ministry at eight, meeting at nine, that is what is planned, and that is what will happen. It is, of course, nonsense to think that everything will work out fine, as he has sworn to Emma.

His words sounded resigned. Adam is not crazy, he is prepared, he has explored all the escape routes, has all the excuses ready, every connection with the conspirators against Hitler has been erased. Emma, believe me, they won't dare to take anyone from Foreign Affairs, not Adam, not me.

Emma lays her hand on his chest. Her fingers briefly drum on the place where his heart is, lightly, softly. Then, very carefully, she lies on top of him. She tucks him in like a child, nothing remains but his eyes and his breath. And hers. Five o'clock, six, six thirty, hours of a life that is over. Emma and Carl get up, put on their clothes mechanically, hear the sounds of the street, sounds of a degenerate day.

"Tell Adam to come and visit again soon, I've kept his favorite jam for him."

A sentence from a little stage play, empty and without context.

Carl nods. "Indeed I will."

From the front door to the street: garden path, raspberry bush, gate, turn left. Emma watches him go, like a puppet disappearing behind a curtain, controlled by an invisible hand. Through Dahlem, down into the U-Bahn, underneath the ruined city, up the stairs to the meeting room, where Adam looks up from his papers.

Their handshake, the questions on their faces.

7

"Judith?"

She felt the nurse's hand on her shoulder and saw a ring on one of the fingers.

"A ring at the end of his nose, his nose, a ring at the end of his nose."

Judith gave her patient a look of concern. What she was saying certainly sounded confused. She seemed young yet old at the same time, lucid yet troubled, a boat adrift.

Emma deftly dabbed the cracker crumbs from her plate with a wet finger. As happy as a little girl, to look at her.

The nurse had no idea.

What had Bruno said about the street where he had spent the war? That there had been a fence around it, that the rules that applied there were unknown elsewhere, and of no use. Sometimes a rumor of war drifted down the street, but there was little reaction.

The street was surrounded by roads and alleyways, a sailing lake, a school, a wood nearby, and it looked insignificant, a street like so many others. All in all, that little street was no more than an elongated block of flats, three stories high, with maybe eighty or ninety people living there. Most were young, with small children or babies or some on the way. But insignificant, no, not that. Ferry, the womanizer, lived there with his wife, Dietje; Henri, the local hero, and his wife, Pauline; Hein, the judge, and his wife, Ank; Erik and his wife, Ruut, who had hidden people during the war; Jan, the lawyer, married to Anneke; Maarten, the philosopher, and his wife, Maria; René, the homosexual, and his boyfriends. And Bruno. The blank, the man on his own, who cycled to the offices of the Peterson Shipping Company every morning, to a life outside this sheltered idyll.

Step by step, the details of his street had made their way into Emma's life. Bruno did not talk about those years easily, or often. But at the dance night at the club he is quite open with her.

With a degree of haste, he tells Emma stories that will remain with her, about that peculiar, closed-off little world, five years under a bell jar of illusions and repression. She just listens, makes no comment, why would she? She knows all about illusions and repression, her years in that well-to-do neighborhood in Berlin were just the same.

Emma listens as if her future depends on it. The music the band is playing is from before the war. Everything that is reliable, everything that still works, seems to be from before the war. Almost a year has passed since liberation, and people are actually beginning to get used to peace.

As the evening comes to an end, Chris Dudok and his group are among the last to leave. The musicians pack up their instruments, a cover goes over the piano, the barman announces the last round, the room becomes emptier and emptier. Bruno and Emma stand slightly to one side, beneath a giant painting of a group of men around a table looking sternly into the room.

"Our very own Sampling Officials," says Bruno cheerfully, a reference to Rembrandt's painting. "The man in that chair there is Imke's father, a doctor, the others may have wanted to sit as well, but presumably there weren't any other chairs in the studio. Look, there, to the left of the center, that's old Dudok, Chris' father, with the high starched collar."

Emma looks up and realizes that the man must be her mother's brother. She saw him a few times when she was young, but never since. She cannot remember her mother having much contact with the "rich branch" of the Dudoks. Feigning a serious expression, she studies the monstrously large painting.

"Isn't your father in it, Bruno?"

"No, my father wasn't one for clubs and societies and all those cliques. A mayor doesn't have any friends, that was one of the things he liked to say. My mother ignored him, though, and regularly organized meals with her friends. He'd happily flout his own rules to join them, and then dominate the table."

Sampling officials, cliques, societies, bowling clubs, bridge drives, the rowing association, a long list of ordinary things in a world that was strange: for much of her life, Emma had not been part of such groups. Far away from all the fun and the family stories, she had found herself in the Berlin of the late 1930s, the very opposite of conviviality. But it was where Carl lived, Carl Regendorf, the man who . . . Stop. Don't do that, don't think, not backward, not back there. Stand beneath the painting, and listen to the pleasant voice of someone she has never met before, but who is the first person since Carl that she finds interesting, maybe even attractive.

"May I take you home? I'm staying with friends not far from you, it's more or less on my way." The question sounds like an apology.

A little later, Chris and his wife Imke, and Bruno and Emma are crossing the marketplace toward Kattensingel. As they pass the town hall, Bruno points out the window of his father's office. Even with its colored stained-glass window, it looks gloomy, a little prison cell.

"'The command post'—that's what my father called his room. He liked to speak telegram-style, military, abrupt. Used as few verbs as possible. He spoke like an officer to disguise his gentle nature—that's what I always thought. God, I loved that man."

Chris chimes in: "Your father's already a legend in the city. Did you know that, Bruno?"

He nods, yes, yes, he knows. His father, the one-eyed officer, former soldier in the Royal Netherlands East Indies Army, wounded during a crackdown against rebels in the interior of Aceh.

"His main adversary in the council was a man called Staal. And Staal became an alderman last week. Your father must be spinning in his grave, Bruno. Staal, even the name of the man! Steel. A dyed-in-the-wool communist, made your father's life as mayor a misery. That's what did for him, Bruno, I'm telling you, that man hounded him until he became ill and then died. I'm not joking."

Bruno does not reply. Chris is speaking more to Emma than to him.

"Emma, you know, where we're walking now, it was packed with people eight years ago. The whole square was literally black, everyone was wearing mourning bands and ribbons. Bruno's father was taken from the town hall to his 'final resting place,' as the newspaper put it. Resting place, a fine expression. It was incredibly quiet on the marketplace. I was there. But at one point a man cried out, in a furious, threatening voice: 'Staal!' It boomed over the square, and everyone became even quieter."

Bruno glances at Emma. He touches the bandage on his ear, shifts it a little, starts to say something, but bites his tongue. Their footsteps echo across the almost-empty marketplace.

Then Emma asks him if what Chris said is right. She was already living in Berlin, she heard barely anything about the Netherlands and what was happening there, let alone in Gouda.

"Yes. Yes. Staal. The name was spoken as little as possible at home, because we all knew how he'd got under my father's skin. My father, who was scared of no one, had to concede defeat to that streetfighter, Staal. It really rankles that he's an alderman now. But he must have been on the right side during the occupation, eh, Chris?"

"Staal? During the occupation? To be honest, I don't know."

Good, bad, neutral, brown, black, weak, obedient, obliging, head in the sand, deaf. Emma has learned all the nuances in the descriptions of who to celebrate or condemn. But she herself is outside such language, outside all such distinctions, she is a category apart. She was married to a "good German," whatever that might mean.

She never talks about it, even though she has told Chris and Imke, as she had no choice. Chris had been extremely interested in her story. He kept coming back to the bombings, to everyday life in Germany, asking her again and again how it was possible for so many people to emerge alive from the rubble. And if she had known anyone in Hamburg or Dresden or Lübeck.

Lübeck? No, Carl had always lived in Berlin, or abroad, his family came from the south.

8

Up five flights of granite steps, past doors with a light-brown varnish, to the top floor, flat 6. B. VERWEIJ is written on a business card loosely tucked into the corner of a small mirror in the middle of the door.

"Mister?" Emma says, pointing at the card.

"*Meester*, Master of Laws, but it's not serious or contagious. Come on in, you got up here faster than I thought, I saw you coming and I was just about to go down to open the door."

"Someone was coming out, so I slipped in. Funnily enough, the man who held open the door said: 'Are you here to see Bruno Verweij?' Did you warn everyone I was coming, Bruno?"

"We always have a meeting beforehand to discuss whether a new person is allowed into the street. Our front door is the closest to the border with the rest of the world, so we take the first hits. But no one spoke out against you, they said you could come in. Someone did ask what you did in the war though. But I didn't know, and luckily they turned a blind eye."

Comic act for two uncertain people.

A few weeks after the dance night in Gouda, Bruno had plucked up the courage to invite Emma to his home.

Unexpectedly, she had said yes. And so here she is. In the place where he has lived alone for six years now, a flat of sixty square meters at most, on the third floor and on a corner, with a view of a school, a patch of grass, a canal covered with duckweed. There are sailing boats on a lake in the distance. Light enters the rooms on three sides. When the sun is shining and the shades are down, everything seems to be bathed in gold.

That is how it is in May 1946 as he leads the way to the balcony, where he has put out coffee and cups and biscuits.

"Did you bake them yourself, Bruno? You don't need a wife!"

He laughs, soft, infectious, and she joins in. A small table, two chairs, that is about all that will fit on the balcony. There is also a ladder leading up through a hatch onto the flat roof.

"An escape route for rejected women," he says, maintaining the same humorous tone, when she asks what the hatch is for.

"Oh, then shall I just . . . ?"

"Not before trying this delicious coffee and a biscuit I bought with coupons I saved up myself."

The tone, the atmosphere, the masquerade of nonchalance and jokes, suddenly Emma recognizes the early days with Carl—that is how it was then, that is how it is now, it is good and will remain so.

"So no future wife, then?"

"The only visitor who's ever gone up through that hatch was a man from the Resistance, certainly no women. Frits Rauwenhoff was his name, a neighbor who had come round to see me. I didn't even realize he was in the Resistance until the police rang the doorbell and he zipped up onto the roof and vanished. The raid was a failure, they never caught him. Clever chap, he knew very well that I was the only one in this block with a ladder up to the roof. After liberation, he came round to thank me. Nonsense, I said, I'm the one who should be thanking you. Turns out he was an important squad leader."

Then Bruno apologizes for bringing up the war.

"So, to get back to your question, no, no future wife, not yet. But I've been working on it for the past few weeks. Constantly. Day and night. It's a tough job."

A curious declaration of love. Emma cannot help laughing out loud. The way he said it, it was so awkward and yet so funny. The grinning face of a neighbor pops up from the next balcony.

"Clear off, Maarten, get back in your hole. Yes, this is a woman. Yes, she's laughing—and no, it's no business of yours."

"Welcome to the street, Emma!" the man says and is gone.

Something that has begun so well has to end well too, he thinks, he hopes, he tells her later.

"How does he know my name, Bruno?" she says.

"I talk in my sleep, and the walls are thin."

The witticisms tumble over one another, dancing between them, as Bruno and Emma keep each other at a distance, for as long as it takes.

And that is a long time, a few weeks already, with months still to go.

The contours of Emma's life remain vague, she fends off everything to do with the war years, and, even before that, with her childhood. Bruno has found out little more than that she was married to a German, lived in Berlin and fled because of something connected to her husband, but she does not tell him any details, avoids the subject.

Berlin, marriage, betrayal and escape, these are ghostly concepts that make Bruno's own history pale into insignificance.

Being in love with Maarten's wife for nearly three years, and their underground relationship that took place in cellars and closets, in the wood and on the little islands in the lake, suddenly feels childish, almost infantile, even though having to give her up in the last year of the war threw him off balance for many months. The emptiness without her. He does not tell Emma anything about that either, she finds out only much later.

Their stories are full of holes, and yet they like what they hear more and more each time.

9

"It's Monday today, isn't it, Judith?"

"Yes, that's right."

"So he's coming tomorrow."

"Mm, at eleven o'clock, he said."

Asking over and over what day and time it is—the mantra of a woman who is rapidly running out of time.

A week before, Emma had stopped eating, stopped taking her medication, and she was drinking less and less. The euphemistic term was "letting go of life," a method of dying that was as old as humankind. Had her grandmother not done much the same? She remembered her father once telling her about it. How he had supported his mother, who had threatened to throw herself out of the window if he did not help her, and how it had haunted his dreams. Assistance with letting go of life. Now, it was Emma's son Thomas' turn to come from Germany, where he had been living for years.

Her father. A ghost in a realm from which there is no return. Her father, Oscar Verschuur, had been a lifelong diplomat and a lifelong fugitive, forever traveling to far-off capitals. Without a photograph, Emma had difficulty bringing his face to mind, and she certainly could not recall the sound of his voice. And yet, even with all his mystery, he did not escape her memory for a moment.

There had been times when Emma could hardly bear him, as he was so far beyond her reach. But, despite all his evasion, she had loved him terribly, almost excessively, or at least help-lessly. That love remained, he was a distant compass, and yet still so close.

Even now, in her final days, he was there. Emma was aware of his approval or disapproval, and when she made her deci-sion to stop eating she wondered what he would have thought. Emma's father watched over her shoulder, but that was never a problem.

"That's fine, Emma," he would likely have said.

Fine, fine. Everything that received the stamp of approval was "fine."

But what exactly made it fine, what invisible guidelines from which unknown god? Decency, indifference, compla-cency, tolerance. The fineness of mediocrity or impotence? It was an unfathomable criterion: something was either "fine" or it was not.

Emma's father had died very suddenly at the beginning of February 1953, and with no obvious cause. Dying during the disastrous floods of '53 was anything but "fine," your death notice was lost among so many others. Martinus Nijhoff, another of her heroes, had died in the same week. Emma had asked for one of his lines to be printed on Oscar's mourning card: *To live is to dream, and death, I think, is what awakens us.*

There were not many people at the funeral. Oscar's friends were scattered all over the world. And Emma's mother Kate was not there to bury her husband, she was traveling in Africa, Emma had been unable to contact her. It was only when she returned to the Netherlands that she heard Oscar was dead and buried.

A gray morning at Westerveld cemetery, dunes full of distinguished gravestones, family crypts almost the size of houses, statues among weeping willows. The strong wind has blown the flowers from the graves, the potted plants and wreaths and ribbons brought by visitors are scattered all around, the gardeners are busy tidying up. Emma walks at the front with Bruno, who is holding Michael and Thomas by the hand. A small procession follows behind.

It is as if she has to be both wife and daughter.

The small children find it interesting, they whisper and Thomas even sings occasionally. The walk through Westerveld takes a long time, too long for her liking, up the dunes, down the dunes. Emma has not yet seen who is walking behind her. She does not look around until they are standing beside the grave, in a circle as best they can. She sees unfamiliar faces, recognizes a few old friends, retired diplomats, some distant relations, Chris and Imke, of course. And then, directly opposite, on the other side of the circle, the most distant from her, her father's most trusted friend. Emma has not seen him since the war. Mr. Wapenaar, Adriaan Wapenaar. Wherever did he come from? Emma nods at him, he does the same back at her.

His presence upsets Emma's carefully composed equilibrium of grief and responsibility. She wants to commemorate her father without too much emotion. Out in the open air, with wind gusting through the bushes and trees, it is already a challenge, but Wapenaar constitutes an actual threat. He is connected to the most devastating years of her life, the part she has always kept silent about. She wants to say something, but no sound comes from her throat. Wapenaar gives her a nod of encouragement. No one seems to notice, not even Bruno.

Then Emma speaks, briefly, intensely. She mentions her mother, whom she was sadly unable to reach—no one seems to think that strange, although it certainly is, even though her parents had been separated for so long. Now and then she looks at Wapenaar, who is listening, motionless, his head gently tilted. Should she refer to him as her father's brother-in-arms? That is what she had been planning to do, not suspecting that he would be present.

She does so and, within a few sentences, the lost, loathed city of Berlin penetrates their circle, along with the love and friendship that she experienced there in spite of everything.

Oscar Verschuur and Adriaan Wapenaar, two of a kind, before the war, during the war and after. Two drifters, always on the move. What remained was their alliance, their respect for each other's secrets. Her father had considered their friendship a sort of life insurance. Rightly so.

Wapenaar stares at the ground.

"They took him to . . . Emma, he was . . . he . . ."

Wapenaar puts his hand on her shoulder, his wife Elka holds both of Emma's hands. At the table in the conservatory, the blood freezes in her head, she feels nothing, her eyes are shut, her body is closed, in the garden a dog barks and barks. Where are her father and mother, they are never there when you need them.

They are nowhere, just like now, just like here, on a bare and windy Wednesday morning in this godforsaken cemetery by the North Sea. Emma is terrified that she will have to stop speaking. Wapenaar in her field of vision, struggling with his tears, is simply too much to bear.

Bruno lets go of the boys' hands and puts his arm around her, just in time. She thanks everyone for coming, invites them all to have a drink with the family, walks to the coffin beside the open grave, lays her hand on it for a moment, turns to face Wapenaar and nods.

He waited until the line of people offering their condolences had dissolved. Bruno has taken the boys outside, the sun is coming out.

"Hello, Emma, your father would have been proud." Wapenaar hugs her, something he has never done before.

"Mr. Wapenaar, I wasn't expecting you to come. I hope it was alright, what I said about my father and you."

"Oscar has the status of a hero among diplomats, Emma, you probably never realized. I heard on the diplomatic grapevine that he'd died. While most of us stayed at our desks, he was helping people over the border into Switzerland, which was unspeakably dangerous. He never said much about it himself, but after the war all kinds of stories came out about his clever and successful missions in the mountains. Your father was an exceptionally courageous man, Emma. I admired him tremendously."

"But you did the same in Berlin, Mr. Wapenaar. You may even have been in greater danger than my father. You must be at least as much of a legend."

A contest in fame and bravery. Wapenaar brushes it off.

"I see you've remarried and have children now. What wonderful news. Elka will be delighted."

"How is she, Mr. Wapenaar? Would you send her my warmest greetings?"

"She sends hers to you too. She's seriously ill, or she would certainly have been here."

Wapenaar says it in a flat voice. Emma takes his arm, he lays his hand on hers. The same move repeated, hand on shoulder on arm, but this time without Elka.

She is back in Grunewald, in the Wapenaars' conservatory.

Emma asked the nurse to take her to bed. The cracker had been digested, the cavity inside was expanding. She was beyond hunger, and she felt barely any thirst. Now and then she raised a glass to her mouth, but she did not drink, just moistened her lips.

She did notice, though, that her memory was becoming overloaded. Emma wandered through her recollections along a complex network of corridors, the crumpled map of her life.

She was ninety-six years old, she had witnessed a century, and understood nothing at all.

10

It really does take months. Bruno catches the train from Rotterdam to Gouda—as often as is wise, he does not want to scare her off—because he does not own a car. Chris does, though, and Emma is allowed to borrow it whenever she wants. Sometimes she surprises him. She waits in Bruno's street until he comes home from work, and watches as he gracefully takes the corner from Oudedijk and cycles toward her.

Summer 1946, a year after liberation, a year after Emma came stumbling into the country. The slow but sure transition to a normal life, the kind of life she knew about but had entirely lost, or at least pushed into the background.

The world of her childhood, of her grandparents, and of her parents when they were still a family and lived in Ireland, Belgium, America and Brazil. As a child she had played in all those countries, she had been to school there, and had always found it easy enough to move to yet another new city and yet another new schoolteacher. With her parents there, nothing bad could happen to her. Until, that is, she was left behind in Leeuwarden, at her grandparents' house. That ice-cold moment when her father and mother went away, "for her own good."

More than twenty years later, her voice still trembles as she tells Bruno about this. Telling stories is not really her strong point. Every story comes from a long way off, is slow to get going, conceals more than it reveals, but that does not bother them, they are in no hurry. They are sitting on the balcony, looking out at the sailing boats on the lake.

The summer months of '46 are warmer than ever before, they stay out on the balcony until late, the lights off inside, Bruno brings first tea, then port and red wine. Advances on tiptoe, as if they have to sound out everything all over again: their pasts, their memories, their bodies, their desire. A strange dance with motionless feet, a standing shuffle like their first encounter at De Reünie. On the dance floor by the billiards table, his hand on her hip, the beginning of the change, the chaos over, out and away from Carl's love.

"There's something I'd like to show you, but I'm afraid you'll have to climb the ladder."

Bruno's face in the setting sun looks weathered, bothered. The ladder to the hatch in the flat roof. He opens it, climbs through, and holds out his hand to help Emma up the last part, an awkward approach to a panoramic view. The roof is covered with rough gravel. In the middle, at fixed distances, square chimneys, beacons marking cozy homes with open fireplaces.

Bruno does not let go of Emma's hand and walks a few feet from the edge. It is easy to feel giddy with all that empty space around you, he says, it has happened to him several times up on that roof. They stop by one of the chimneys, and he points at the city, at the world of others.

The most intimate light of all falls in September, at its softest around six or seven in the evening. A neighbor across the way calls his pigeons home. As if on a lasso, the birds glide in loops above his head, before descending, one by one, into their loft. A pigeon fancier's circus trick. Emma and Bruno watch as the last pigeon exits the stage. The outstretched arms of cranes, a church tower, the chimney of a gasworks sticking up in the distance. Rotterdam is still flat, the Witte Huis is the tallest building in the country, and with binoculars you can look out over half the city.

"What do you think of our street down there?" he says.

Our street?

"Would you like to stay here with me?"

Bruno looks at Emma, and she looks at him. She sees the bandage on his ear, she has never seen him without it, feels the grip of his hand, notices how he wants to keep them both in balance.

She lays her other hand on his cheek.

11

"Mr. B. Verweij, Deputy Secretary, Chamber of Commerce and Industry, Rotterdam" it says on his card. Freshly printed, an admission ticket to adulthood. Chamber of Commerce, it sounded like a society from the Golden Age. And a Golden Age will come again, and this time the victory will begin here, in Rotterdam.

Bruno travels with his boss, K.P. van der Mandele, to Germany. Goes with K.P. to Hamburg and Lübeck, Krefeld and Cologne, Düsseldorf, along the Rhine, down the Elbe. K.P., the initials of an ace, a professional, in the war it was also the abbreviation used for the *knokploegen*, the armed Resistance squads. And it suits him, K.P.'s a tough guy: K.P. fights his way along the German rivers, with Rotterdam behind him, and Bruno Verweij at his side.

Bruno's apprenticeship. Forgotten are the dark days at the Peterson Shipping Company, at a time when the port was barely functioning, was a war zone, a waypoint for the enemy and for neutrals: Swiss, Portuguese, Swedes and South Americans.

Van der Mandele and Bruno have become unwitting pioneers of reconciliation. From those crushed German towns and cities, trade is once again slowly moving out onto the water, Rotterdam is becoming a synonym for prosperity, for the supply of everything they no longer have.

The German businessmen scarcely dare to hope that anyone will want to talk to them. K.P. and Bruno do so, but more for the sake of the Rotterdammers than for the Germans. The Chamber is the most civilized way to get business back on track.

Bruno does not always know quite what to think about traveling around that despised country and being welcomed so warmly. Is it alright simply to shake hands there, to have meetings, to go to receptions and dinners? For now, the Americans are paying for it all, there is nothing in place yet, but everything smells of the future. Germany has to be helped back onto its feet, that is how they will keep the Russians at bay. Battlefield Europe needs to be cleaned up as quickly as possible: the desert shall blossom as the rose.

Emma and Bruno blossom, too. Their two sons, Michael and Thomas, born a year apart, play with the other children out on the street. It is the 1950s. Half the world is in scaffolding, there is a sound of hammering and sawing wherever you go.

But in the middle of this period of blossoming, Bruno's mother dies, on a July day in 1950. She made it through the war so well, and her death is unexpected.

As a four-, five-, six-year-old, Bruno had often lain under the piano like a dog while his mother played Chopin, or Liszt's "Liebestraum," the most beautiful music he knew—it had become the theme of his life. But the ridicule of his brothers, their comments about the baby hiding beneath his mother's baby grand, eventually drove him from his favorite spot, and he had sat beside her on the piano stool instead.

They set out for Zeeland straightaway, making it to her bedside just in time. Bruno, his brother Hendrik, along with his wife, their little girl, Maud, who had been bombed into a wheelchair by a British attack, and Emma.

"When is Rob coming?" their mother asks just before she dies.

"He's on his way, Mother, he should be here any minute." Bruno looks at Hendrik, they both know he is lying. Their brother Rob, conspicuous by his absence, left the continent even before the war, in search of something that does not exist. Juggler of his own fate, the boy for whom their mother has been waiting fifteen years. They found him eventually, he had moved house several times, and they sent him money to pay for his journey from Cape Town, where he was apparently based at that point.

He is not going to make it, they realize. He will be too late, will not see their mother again. Their brother, their neglected shadow, their guilty conscience.

He still comes though, confounding everyone's expectations. Too late, admittedly. As if he wanted to protect his mother from himself. Bruno waits for him in the arrivals hall at Schiphol. He spent hours out on the huge viewing platform overlooking the runways, the K.L.M. airplane from South Africa is endlessly delayed. Bruno is the one who still receives the occasional sign of life from Rob, a few letters about how he had "rolled through" the war. They were the letters of a showman, although full of horrors. Tales about the Burma railway line he had worked on, and the torpedoing of the transport ship that was to have taken him and two thousand others to Nagasaki. About the atomic bomb that had fallen close to his camp. About Manila, Batavia and Cairo, about his return to South

Africa. Rob had described everything with the casual good cheer of a survivor. But under every line Bruno had sensed the sadness, and the defeat.

In his last letter, which came a few weeks before their mother's death, there had been nothing but a photograph: Rob with two strangers in front of a life-sized poster at a cinema in some unknown city. Rob in the middle, in a white dinner jacket, pointing at the title of the film: "'Til We Meet Again." Someone next to Rob was pointing at the picture of the leading lady.

Bruno had given the photograph to his mother. She had said nothing, but after she died they found it in her diary, fastened with a paperclip to the date of her death.

"'Til We Meet Again"—the story of a man who searches for his beloved in the underworld, the song of a woman who must not look back, but who does so anyway.

When the large glass doors have closed behind him, Rob looks aimlessly around, his face white from the lack of sleep. Bruno approaches him tentatively, scarcely believing it is his brother standing there. He has not seen him for fifteen years, since he waved him off at Hook of Holland. In 1935, a world war ago.

"Little brother?"

The incredulity is mutual. The awkward, almost shamefaced reunion of two brothers who have disappeared from each other's lives, sons of a mother who has just departed.

Fellow passengers stop a porter to take their luggage, one slaps Rob on the shoulder as he walks by, says "cheers." Rob laughs, calls something after him in Afrikaans, takes Bruno's arm and starts walking. Or something that approximates walking.

Bruno leads him outside as best he can, but it is a risky undertaking. Rob's legs more or less refuse to work, something inside is blocked.

Bruno later tells Emma how shocked he was by that first sight of his brother, those first steps. And he repeats, word for word, the conversations they had had. Bruno's story would never leave Emma and, though his end was tragic, the light of those few days remained and that last evening with Rob, her long-lost brother-in-law, her newfound ally.

"A body that's all dead weight, Emma."

"He needs to see a doctor, Bruno. I'll ask Dr. Milders to take a look at him."

Rob had just stared at them as though he had long been aware that it was too late for a doctor. The bomb had done a thorough job. A body carrying five years of nuclear fallout, a degree in medicine is not needed to arrive at the correct diagnosis. Cancer, from head to toe. Although Dr. Milders had not expressed himself in those terms after receiving the test results. He had merely inquired again about his patient's symptoms, intent, concerned.

"Of a transitory nature, doctor. I'm referring to myself, of course. How long have I got?"

Milders had stood up.

"Not long. Six months, maybe a year."

Rob shook him by the hand: "You're an optimist! Thank you for your time, please send the bill to my brother—he insists. That lad needs to take better care of himself, by the way. I'm rather worried about *his* health. Have you seen those ears of his?"

12

The evening before his flight leaves, Rob's old Dutch friends all meet up in Bruno and Emma's street. Most of them are female.

One last evening without a body and without a war, he must have thought. He does not mention what the doctor has said, he does not say anything, not even to Emma and Bruno. Three months later, when he is found dead in Cape Town, Milders tells them about the result of his examination, and about Rob's reaction.

They come from Gouda and Gorkum and Amsterdam and Deventer, young, married, mothers, and Bruno and Emma, of course. Their brother Hendrik is not there, too busy, he sent his apologies. Rob and Bruno know what their brother's "too busy" means—with Rob there, his old envy has reared its head again, the adventurer's magnetism annoys Hendrik, always has done.

Rob has done up the basement as a bar. Lanterns in the dark hallway cast just enough light for them to see one another. A steep staircase leads down to the concrete rooms with the bicycles and the rubbish bags, and there is a narrow corridor connecting the residents' storage spaces. It could have served as an air-raid shelter.

Rob has borrowed a gramophone and bought drinks, or rather, Emma has. There are records from the 1930s—German, Viennese, British, American. And liberation music, tunes from the Great American Songbook, Cole Porter, Tommy Dorsey's band, Bing Crosby.

Rob knows every note of every song, and he sings along. And he tells his life story, his years in the Indies and the Far East and South Africa. The magic he once possessed in the company of women now comes back. They are as enchanted as ever by his tales and by his voice. In everything he says they sense his wild sophistication, his dislike of the mundane, his disturbing charm. And his loneliness. It is an alluring cocktail—for those who dare.

That night, everyone dares. It is summer and warm. Neighbors come from all around to join the gathering, they bring bottles and glasses, and it turns into a party for the whole street. What began with twenty people ends with sixty. A woman takes off her blouse and dances, calm and carefree, in her brightly colored bodice above a white skirt. Rob holds her by one hand, stands motionless as she spins around him. His eyes sparkle when the others applaud.

An hour underground counts for two, the lanterns go out one by one, drawing the darkness inside, but the morning is not far away and there is also a moon. Rob is the center, and yet he is on his way out. None of the women would ever forget this night with Rob, and the same was true of the men. The woman who removed her blouse was not trying to seduce him. She was acknowledging who he is, or who he was. A tribute to the man who was once her lover, the lover of her dreams. Truly a dream, as Rob never stayed, not with anyone.

Someone puts new candles in the lanterns, small points of light return. A gleaming disc spins on the gramophone, they can scarcely hear the music in the crowded corridor. Bruno comes to sit beside Rob.

"You left without a suitcase, and you came back with nothing. Why was that, Rob? I never understood why you left so suddenly, I never had the chance to ask. There were times when I missed you terribly."

His words take Rob away from the party. He turns his head, tries to reply, caught unawares by the sound of Bruno's voice and the emotion in it.

"Father thought I was no good, Hendrik was jealous, you were studying, and Mother..." Rob pauses. "The way you stood there waving on the quay at Hook of Holland, Bruno. You were all there. Do you remember me holding up the letters of recommendation that Father had written for me, tearing them in two, as if I didn't care, and throwing them into the harbor while you were all watching? I never forgave myself for that. It was such a mean, aggressive thing to do and I was nothing but a bumptious brat. If I'd had a pistol, I'd have been waving it around. Don't touch me, leave me alone. I needed to start from scratch, I was going to show the world. My God, it was such a lousy act of rebellion against Father."

Bruno shakes his head, filled with disbelief and impatience. He is struggling to keep his temper.

"We had it good, but you took that great big motorcycle of yours, the one that impressed the girls so much, the same women who are here tonight, and you drove it straight through our family. After you left, I never really saw Father and Mother take pleasure in anything ever again. You didn't get in touch, didn't write, you weren't there when Father died, I had the feeling you'd archived us away for good."

"I couldn't breathe when Father was around. I looked up to him so much, the way I loved him though, it was completely un-realistic. I imitated him, and slowly but surely I began to drift away from him. It was self-preservation, Bruno. But less than eight years later I was crawling through Thailand, along the Burma railway, in a cloud of poisonous flies. So much for self-preservation."

Bruno is furious, Rob sounds bitter, and the plane is leaving for Cape Town that day. As if summoned, Emma appears.

"Emma, your husband's angry with me, please come and join us!"

"But Rob, that's impossible. He's only ever said nice things about you, he shows off about you, in fact. There's no one he's more proud of."

"Doesn't seem like it, Emma. He just gave me a real tongue-lashing."

Rob puts his hands up.

Bruno laughs at his brother's gesture of helplessness, his anger is over.

Rob's night is almost at an end. People are leaning wearily against walls and parked bicycles. Bruno and Emma see what no one else could know: the final hours of a life that never came to fruition, Rob's life. There is no trace of bitterness, only a strange acceptance of his death, which is now not so far off. The three of them neither mention nor deny it. The approaching end does not come between them, but unites them.

For Emma, Rob is new, she knows him only from the stories that Bruno and the others have passed on. Excited stories about a boy who would not be told. A restless man, an adventurer, a fortune-seeker, a prodigal son. A prodigal brother.

Rob, Bruno and Emma stand with glasses in their hands, the men smoke cigarettes, they are fully equipped to survive the party.

The warmth lingers in the basement, it has barely cooled down this evening. The blouseless woman walks up to Rob, puts her arm around his neck.

"You going to take me with you to Cape Town?" she asks, in a surprisingly serious tone. It is more of a command than a question.

"Of course I'll take you, Anna. But I'm leaving tomorrow, will you manage that?"

Anna will not manage it. She is beautiful, flushed, and a little tipsy.

With his free hand, Bruno gently pushes the woman aside, toward the makeshift bar, afraid that she wants to start a meaningful conversation with Rob. Emma takes Rob by the arm and makes a move to take him upstairs, to their flat. Morning has already broken.

"No, Emma, wait a moment, I'll come up soon, but there's something I'd like to say first. Could you turn off the music?"

He claps his hands, someone calls for silence. From the space around the stairwell the last guests crowd into the room with the drink and the gramophone. Bruno sits on a large heating pipe. Emma clutches Rob's arm, he rests his other arm on the bar.

"Speech, speech!" the voices echo along the hallway. Packed in together, exhausted, eyes glassy but glad, the group looks at Rob, who has appeared like a ghost from their past.

"Two weeks ago my mother was buried. I got here too late, you probably heard. I've arrived everywhere too late for fifteen years, and maybe I should never have left. But that thought has come too late as well. It's not too late to thank all of you for this party, though—you coming here after all these years has made up for a lot. I've thought about you at times. The world where I was, it was deep underground, or close to the ground, or in the hold of a ship, or in a barracks. But yes, sometimes you came to mind, at unexpected moments, and in strange countries. All of you here in the Netherlands were an island that was beyond my reach, an island I had run away from. Only Bruno knows why, and his lips are sealed. My dear friends, what I wanted to say—um . . ."

Rob hesitates, searching for words. Then he looks at Emma, as if she might know what he means to say.

"What I wanted to say is: take care of Emma, a wonderful woman. And of my brother, a wonderful man. I'm going to miss you all."

That is it, he does not say anything else. It is enough. Emma leads Rob through the cellar, along the corridor, up the stairs. He hugs everyone, laughs, kisses the women, and then again. Footstep by footstep, slowly upward, to his bed, to Cape Town.

Just as Bruno had fetched him, he also takes him back to the airport. The difference is that Rob now has a suitcase with him, filled with the silverware from their childhood home. He chose it when they divided up the inheritance. "Something that can fit inside just one suitcase," was his guideline. The best silver, they had always eaten with it, bits of memory.

"Rob can choose first," Bruno had said. "And no silly knick-knacks, it has to be something expensive."

Rob has enough difficulty lifting the suitcase, so walking with it is impossible. Bruno takes it, more or less pushes Rob along and hands him over to a stewardess, who will accompany him.

"My pieces of silver," Rob says, pointing at the suitcase.

Bruno smiles, but it is not heartfelt.

"Take care of yourself, little brother, and get something done about those ears of yours, the bandage doesn't seem to be helping."

"I'll try, Rob. Let us know when you get home. Take care."

"Yeah, yeah, Bruno, you'll be the first to hear. Fine, nurse, let's go."

The stewardess does not protest when he puts his arm around her shoulders. She gives him a look of cheerful concern.

Rob turns around one more time before he goes through passport control.

"Take care of Emma, Bruno!"

And he is gone.

When Bruno tells Emma about the scene at Schiphol, he asks her, with a pretense of envy, what she and Rob had been talking about.

"You made quite the impression on him. His last words were about you!"

13

"Oh, Judith, I'd rather like to get up, it must be morning by now. I have to look halfway decent for Thomas, he'll be here before we know it."

Emma had picked up the old cowbell that was always beside her bed. The ringing could be heard through the wall in the room where the nurse slept.

"No, Mrs. Verweij, it's only three o'clock, you should get a little more sleep, it's still night time."

This time she had stayed in the chair beside Emma's bed, so the bell woke her immediately and she answered straightaway.

Sleep. Emma suddenly felt as if she had been sleeping all her life, as if she had slept through it, in fact. Close to death, she was seized by the conviction that she had barely lived. Ninety-six years old and she had only just woken up.

They really should come up with some better method than sleeping for regaining one's strength. So excessive, eight hours a day in bed, my goodness, what a waste of time. There was a pill for everything these days, but nothing you could take to avoid sleep. Nijhoff was right, it is death that awakens us. She had finally grasped that, but it was a little late in the day.

Tomorrow morning Thomas would come, and then the
"team," a nice word for the beginning of the end. Welcome,
East Rotterdam Sedation Team, welcome indeed.

Emma pictured a brigade of injectors entering the house.
Eager for the fray, fully armed, a radiant gleam in their eyes,
trained in a gentle approach. East Rotterdam Sedation Team
reporting for duty, always willing, always prepared, effective
and at your service. Shadows on the wallpaper, ghosts emerging from the doctor's bag.

Her doctor was a woman. Thomas had managed to replace
the old doctor with a female colleague just in time. The first
doctor preferred not to make house calls, but if he did pay a
visit, he was more interested in the paintings on the wall,
which he stood looking at with his hands in his pockets, than
he was in the old woman who wanted to discuss her ailment
or illness or death. The "no-need-to-worry-your-head-about
-that-my-dear-woman" type.

Emma had put up with it for a long time and had found
his appreciation of her art and her furniture amusing, but in
the light of what was approaching, his avoidance strategy had
begun to annoy her.

The woman was a breath of fresh air. Weekly visits, no dis-
tracting chats about the contents of the flat, she did not look
at anything else, focused solely on her patient's condition.
Because that was what Emma had become after her fall in the
kitchen—a patient. That fall on the kitchen floor had shaken
up her world, pieces of the puzzle had gone flying, the jigsaw in
her head. Her life was unwinding, with strange clarity, but in a
random order.

Her cheek is close to his shoulder and sometimes brushes the
soft fabric of his jacket. He holds the book loosely to one side,

as if to make room for her. He is reading out something from a rather obscure treatise by Kierkegaard. A hundred years on, the Danish magician is once again in the spotlight, because of the work of new existentialists such as Heidegger and Sartre.

The words do not do much for Emma, but the voice reading them does. Louis Terpstra, a pastor who occasionally comes to preach in the city and whom she listens to as if so much were at stake. An older man, attractive for what he knows and how he talks about it, dangerous for a woman whose children have almost left home and whose husband travels a lot. God and eroticism, a fine team. Terpstra knows that too, and for a long time he puts up a brave fight against his feelings.

"One cannot engage with God 'to some extent.' For God is the absolute antithesis of all that is 'to some extent,'" he reads.

Louis repeats the Dane's sentence. It is, of course, true, he says, although he has to confess that he himself has not progressed far beyond "to some extent."

"Well, you've made it all the way here to my sofa, Louis."

He laughs. The sofa they are sitting on is long enough to lie on. There are so many sublime and unfathomable thoughts in the pages they have just worked through that the amazement in Louis' voice kept on rising. They understand the quote from the diary. But Emma is upset by the dogmatism in everything the philosopher wrote. Men and their absolute statements, engraved in bronze, carved in marble. Not to mention their ideas about women. Kierkegaard certainly had that tendency, woman this, woman that, frightened, neurotic, endlessly fascinated by the Woman.

"Judith!"
  "Yes?"
  "Someone called out my name."

"No, they didn't. There's no one here but me."

"Someone laughed, Judith, and I heard a door slam. Has Louis left?"

"You must have been dreaming, or maybe it was a memory. I've never heard you mention a Louis before. Is he family?"

Emma lay with her eyes open, looking into the darkness. She realized that she had indeed been dreaming, but it was the truth. Dreaming the truth, a vague episode had come sailing past, part of everything she had so majestically suppressed.

Louis was just passing through, someone she had once comforted and who had wanted to take her in his arms. "No, Louis, no." He had slammed the door, Kierkegaard lay on the floor. Sweet dreams.

14

It is June 1966 and Bruno is going on a trip, his last with K.P., who is about to retire. D.B., "distinguished bullyboy," as she and Bruno occasionally call him. For two weeks they will travel around a Germany that was rebuilt just as quickly as their own Rotterdam. Both razed to the ground, both bounced back and gleaming with prosperity. D.B. and Bruno had long since stopped feeling furtive as they passed through the cities on the Rhine, no longer felt embarrassed at German receptions. They had made friends and were on first-name terms with their hosts. The offering of first names was a serious business for the Germans, a ritual that involved tears, handshakes, arms around shoulders, and solemn wishes for no more wars.

Back to Germany, time and again. Bruno barely thinks about it now, it has become second nature. Rotterdam is the revolving door to trade with Germany, the Chamber of Commerce is the doorman who ensures that the hinges stay oiled. But how does Emma feel about him spending so much time there? Every time he goes, it is as if he is penetrating the camouflaged hideaway of her past.

For twenty-one years she has not been to that country; for twenty-one years she has not wanted to look in that direction. Occasionally Bruno asked her to come along on one of his trips, but she always found an excuse not to go. Until this time. Hiding behind the children will no longer work, they have left home. So she goes with him.

Emma, with nurse Judith sleepy beside her, awoke in confusion. Louis had appeared in her dream, Bruno was going on a trip, and suddenly she was in Germany, away from Louis' arms, she went with Bruno! But of course, he was her husband. Her second one.

To Germany with Bruno, straight across the landscape that once protected her. Is that her first sensation now that she has passed the border and reads the German words on signs, now that she can hear the language on the streets again? How peculiar. They are old reflexes, unexpressed emotions, concealed, suppressed.

June in Germany is terribly beautiful. The hills they pass through are yellow with rapeseed. They are on their way to Hamburg and Lübeck, the Chamber has had an active presence there for years and Bruno has friends in the two cities. Emma does not know northern Germany, and as long as Berlin remains out of the picture and the Black Forest is not mentioned, she will manage this Hansestadt trip. She thinks.

How old would Carl be if . . . ? Fifty-six, in the prime of his life, an age like a rock that can still easily withstand the waves. Her graveless husband.

Emma has systematically quashed every thought about his fate, living with her back to the neighboring country and never looking over her shoulder. It always worked well. A life filled with children and Bruno, the street, the city, the discovery of Louis Terpstra's God and all the fuss that entailed. Put a lid on the well of the past, and everything's fine, excellent, could not be better.

She remembers the promise she made to herself when she crossed the border into Limburg, the solemn vow never to return to the dark bunker of her past. She had sworn that for the rest of her life she would silently accept and love everything and everyone. Happiness as a task, as a duty, as an attainable objective, a longstanding agreement.

"Are you still there, Judith?"

"Of course, Mrs. Verweij, I'm not going anywhere, I'm perfectly comfortable and I . . ."

Emma had already stopped listening.

Suddenly Carl is back. Not because Emma has finally returned to his fatherland. No, he comes from a direction she would never have expected or imagined.

It is early evening. The guests for the reception of the Dutch delegation are arriving in droves. A boat is going to take the entire party around the harbors of Hamburg and, everywhere on deck, in all the rooms and even on the bridge, immaculately laid tables have been set out for dinner. Seagulls and crows perch on neighboring boats, waiting for scraps. Glasses and knives sparkle in the late light. A sailing dinner-dance makes a change from the usual receptions in drab hotels. Emma and Bruno walk around the tables with a few other Rotterdammers. They point out the name cards beside the plates and try to spot their own.

The boat pulls away from the quay, everyone is on board, they are gathering on the foredeck. The sun is still shining, and there is no wind. Most of the women are wearing hats, the men are in their finest suits.

They are still working on the wharf, cranes lifting their loads, lorries driving back and forth, like a demonstration of faith in the future. The port of Hamburg is just a little brother to Rotterdam, but the cities are carefully eyeing each other. K.P. has already issued a warning: watch out for Hamburg. Watch out. In other words, do not let them catch up with you. But tonight they are celebrating twenty years of friendship between the two ports. With glorious abundance.

"Clarita?"

Emma can hardly believe it, it really is her, she is facing the woman she has not seen since that devastating week in '44, the woman who went with her down into the abyss, down into the deepest hole. Clarita von Trott, Adam's wife. For a moment Emma hesitates, maybe there is still a way out, maybe Clarita will not recognize her. But at that same instant Clarita looks at her with a question on her face, and then her expression changes. She removes her hat, her hair flies free, emotion takes hold, within seconds the years disappear.

Their embrace is a magic circle of grief and expectation that nothing and no one can break through. Clarita. Emma. And that means Adam too. And Carl. The song of death.

Carl, where are you, what were your last thoughts before they murdered you? And Adam, a dark absence in a life that just goes on as if nothing has happened.

The boat sways, musicians take their places, a gong rings out and everyone looks for their tables. Bruno watches their encounter from a distance. He has never heard Emma speak German before. Melodious, a forgotten language, it sounds as if she is comforting the other woman, and the words spoken to Emma sound just the same.

He approaches cautiously, briefly lays a hand on Emma's shoulder.

"I'm going over to sit with D.B., and you two can continue your conversation here. I'll take my place card with me."

Emma simply nods and lets him go, this kind, attentive ghost from another world.

Clarita and Emma sit at the table until the night and the cold draw in over the ship. They barely eat, hold each other tight, smile at the other guests, pluck up courage and, interspersed with silences, relive old memories.

For two hours, three, four.

"I wandered around near Plötzensee prison for days. Adriaan Wapenaar—you knew him too, didn't you?—had forbidden me to leave the house, I was in hiding there. But I didn't care about being arrested, I took the risk, I went out onto the streets.

"I could see the buildings from a distance and I knew Carl was locked up inside one of them. Anyone who went in as a prisoner came out dead. We all knew that, Clarita. How could the men who hanged Carl—and later Adam—go home as normal at the end of every day? Where did they hide their dirty hands, how could they hug their wives, pick up their children? It must have been like living in a big, black hole.

"There was nothing I could do, of course not, they turned me away five times. The last time someone warned me that my actions would only harm my husband. They certainly wouldn't release him, but he might be moved to a camp. It all came down to little things. And, specifically, they were not to be annoyed by some Dutch woman who wanted to see her husband.

"'This is not helping him, just go away. You need to wait, maybe your husband will be pardoned.'

"Pardoned? That was when I knew it was over. No one was ever pardoned, it was a notion from a bygone world. The storm did not blow over, the insanity increased, the hunting and the murdering.

"At some point a prison pastor appeared, I can still remember his name: Harald Poelchau. He told me that Carl was no longer alive, and that he had been brave. I stood there, I waited.

"I was still standing opposite the prison gates when the bodies were loaded onto trucks. I heard the commands, the engines firing up, that determined departure with the enemies of the Reich in the back, and one of them was Carl. I didn't want to go on without him, but I had to. I stood there until the evening, until the Tommies came and the sirens were wailing all over the city. I wasn't scared, I wanted to stay there, right across from the prison, in full sight of all those criminals. I hoped a bomb was going to flatten the place."

Clarita nods. She had hoped for a bomb too, and if it landed on the court where Adam was being tried, so be it. Anything was better than Plötzensee.

"Who was it that betrayed Adam, Clarita? Carl was certain nothing could happen to him. He said Adam had erased all traces, he knew the enemy's tricks and traps better than anyone. His friends could be trusted, he had sent no letters containing anything suspicious. So where did it go wrong?"

The raucous sound of the ship's horn immediately follows the question that Emma has been carrying around for so long. Clarita waits for the captain to finish his little concert and then she answers.

"I didn't find out until years after the war. He had managed to shield all of his connections to the Resistance, Carl was right about that. No one could prove anything, even though he was suspected. But those last few weeks before the assassination attempt, Claus von Stauffenberg regularly came to visit him. Not at the Ministry, but at home. Adam believed only

Von Stauffenberg could carry out the attack that he and his friends had been talking about for months, for years. Claus and he sometimes saw each other twice a day. No one knew about it, even the Gestapo had no idea. Until they found the logbook that Stauffenberg's chauffeur kept. The man had noted down every trip, every visit and how long it lasted. Betrayed by the bookkeeping of a driver who wrote down everything, as he had been instructed to. Without that book, Adam might have survived. I've never got over the fact that a stupid little notebook was the only real evidence. It took me a long time to forgive that driver."

People are dancing inside and Emma points out Bruno, who's whirling around with a German woman on a dance floor surrounded by tables.

"So he's your new husband?"

"Yes. Do you have someone?"

"Not since Adam. It didn't work, I couldn't bear the touch of anyone else's hands."

Hands: another word for life with a man. Carl's hands, until the very end. Bruno's hands, with those damaged nails, harbingers of decay. Hands, not eyes, are the mirrors of a man's soul.

Slowly Emma returns. With Clarita's voice in her ears, everything that has not been said and does not need to be said. That turbulent time, those unfettered years together have resurfaced in the port of Hamburg, and their boat has not sunk, it calmly docks, and the moon casts its pale light over the gangway.

Emma and Bruno stand on deck and wave. Clarita's hand waves back. She does not turn around as she steps into the taxi.

15

"Judith, is your mother still alive?"

"Yes, lucky for me, Mrs. Verweij. She's still young, only fifty-one."

"Do you see much of her?"

"Every week. She's lovely. We sometimes go on holiday together. That's if she can get time off work."

"So what does your mother do?"

"She's an office manager for a big firm of architects. They're a bit like artists, these architects—she always says they might be great at designing buildings but that it would be chaos without her."

"And your father?"

"He died ten years ago. I helped to take care of him until the end. Mother couldn't handle it on her own."

"Is that why you became a nurse?"

There was no reply. Emma understood and asked no more questions. Seeing your mother every week, going on trips together, what a luxury. Back in the prehistoric era she had traveled with her mother and father too. To Brazil, where they went to live, where there was no winter. Always together, always sun. Mythical prehistory, the smell of eternity.

Then she had lost her mother. Was she really her mother? Emma had sometimes had her doubts—they had so very little in common—and she had rarely caught herself thinking fondly of her mother. The feeling had seemed to be mutual.

Kate and Oscar, her parents—she searched her mind for the old days before the estrangement set in. Who had they been?

"Was your mother there when your father died?"

There was no reply. Nurse Judith was asleep, Emma could tell from her steady breathing. Now she was alone. And awake. She watched over the child.

"Emma!"

She recognizes the voice immediately, no one speaks her name as forcefully as her mother. This time there's a good reason. She is standing down in the street and speaking on the intercom: *Emma! It's your mother.*

This is typical of her mother, returning from Africa unannounced, coming straight to Rotterdam, and now Emma has to tell her that her husband is dead. Could a situation be any more peculiar? She races downstairs to open the door.

"I tried to reach you everywhere, Mother. But none of the embassies or consulates knew where you were. Where on earth have you been?"

Her mother is shocked, of course, when she hears of Oscar's death. She cries, briefly, not for long, and soon the questions start coming, along with a hint of indignation about the missed funeral.

She had left for the Congo two months earlier, on some unexplained mission.

"In the region where I was, Emma, they don't have news-papers or telephones. I hadn't even heard anything about the floods either, I only found out on the way back, and you're right, there was no way to reach me. But I told you all that beforehand. You did get my letter, didn't you?"

Emma controls herself. Yes, yes, she got it, but did her mother not receive the messages she had left at her home in Barkston Gardens? No, she hasn't been there, she flew straight from the airport in London to the Netherlands, she needed Oscar.

"What was so urgent, Mother? You only saw each other once in a while."

"It was more often than that, darling. I needed his advice, I wanted to see him, and you too, of course, to discuss some-thing that's been on my mind for years."

Emma thinks everything her mother says is vague. Every-thing is covert, shadowy and a little sad. As a matter of fact, much about her parents' lives has been evasive, enigmatic, without obvious affection. Parents are impenetrable creatures, people you think you know, but who often spend their lives in an entirely different reality.

Emma knew all about that. What would her own children think later about Bruno and her? They knew absolutely noth-ing about Carl, even Bruno only knew a few simple, super-ficial facts. Vagueness piled on top of rumor and speculation, on dreams and suspicions: family history is a constant stream of knowing almost nothing, a scrap of insight here and there, an unintentional discovery. Those who find out and understand something do so by accident. The past is black, her parents', and her own as well. No, it is not black, it is dark. Black suggests there is no solution, there is hopelessness in that word, maybe even dishonesty and deception. With "dark," you cannot help thinking of a possible way out, that one day something might come to light.

"What is it, then, Mother, what is it that's been on your mind all these years?"

She already suspects the answer.

"Barbarossa, still?"

The knife in the back of their life as a family. Barbarossa. Code word for the demarcation line between her father and her mother.

16

"Russians."

It is dark in the compartment, it is dusk outside, they have been traveling all that August day too, although the train was mostly at a standstill. For more than forty-eight hours, they have been sitting in a packed train on the way to Baden Baden, or Stuttgart, or as far as possible into the Black Forest. Escape from Berlin. Lots of children with mothers and without fathers, lots of old people, and a few lost soldiers. Hardly anyone speaks.

"Russians"—a voice in the silence, flat and resigned. Those who are sitting by the window, pressed up against it, look over at the other side of the station, where, for three hours now, they have been waiting for permission to move on. A troop of men in dirty black jackets is sheltering there, in a semi-circle, like cows in a storm, silent, their faces turned to the train. A few soldiers with guns stand close to the rails. The rest of the platform is empty.

Even though Emma is by the window, she keeps her eyes closed. Carl had told her about the Russian prisoners of war being dragged across the entire country, executed for the lightest, slightest offense. She and Carl had spent so much time talking about Operation Barbarossa. Adam had heard from Carl when it was going to happen, they had known about the impending attack on Russia and had done absolutely nothing about it. The secret was too vast—how could they have influenced the Wehrmacht, or Stalin for that matter? Emma had warned her father, though, and later Mr. Wapenaar.

Sandwiched between two wide women on the train seat, she reluctantly remembers her trip with Carl and Adam to Geneva, more than three years ago now. Her father was living in Switzerland at the time. It had been a neutral and indifferent paradise, with people shopping and strolling along the promenade beside a lake full of sailing boats. She is still embarrassed at the thought of it.

The secret of Barbarossa has been overtaken by Carl's death, she does not even feel any regret or sorrow inside that stiflingly hot train compartment. The old terror has evaporated, her fury and disappointment about her elusive father are forgotten, the man who helped refugees to cross the border between France and Switzerland by night, and played the obedient diplomat by day.

The Wehrmacht had marched, Russia was crushed, Germany won on all fronts. Until Stalingrad, until there. Now they were beating a hasty retreat across scorched earth.

Emma is nudged by the old woman beside her, who points at the men outside. But she does not want to look, the men on the platform should not be stared at so shamelessly. She does not see the boy fall, she has her eyes closed, she presses her hands to her ears and barely hears the shot. Everything washes over and around her, every day of the journey, every new hour of the war.

"The way that soldier shot that Russian down," her neighbor says, with the steady voice of an experienced bystander who has seen a good many people fall.

17

"It's twelve years ago now, Emma, and you can't tell me a day's gone by when you haven't thought about it. I was convinced your father had passed on your message, he flew to London specially. Carl had received accurate information from von Trott. But he didn't do it, and that drove a permanent wedge between us. It wasn't just because of that Lara woman that your father and I separated, you know."

"That Lara woman? What do you mean? I never heard Father mention anyone called Lara."

So yes, there had been another woman.

How long did it go on? Her mother speaks about it in passing, as if it is generally known, a thing of the past. Yes, it is certainly a thing of the past. Her father is dead, and she stood by his grave talking about someone she apparently did not know as well as she had thought. She could kick that Lara woman. Her mother too, for that matter.

"Did your father keep it from you? I don't think there was anyone he trusted more than you."

"He never said a word about it, but it's not the kind of thing you talk about to your daughter."

Kate laughs. The conversation is taking a turn she does not like.

Her mother seems to be on the warpath. Suddenly she feels free to talk about things that show her husband in a new and dismal light. Dark clouds, shifting shadows, Oscar Verschuur revisited.

Is it the shock of his passing that has made her mother open up? Why are these issues coming up now, after all those years of silence? Should she be talking like this to her mother barely a fortnight after her father's funeral? It feels as if she has to defend herself and her father, as if they are being called to account.

And yet, looking back on it later, much later, she had felt more empathy for her mother, a woman walking her own path, a brave and lone crusader against injustice, wherever she encountered it.

For Emma, the whole nightmarish Barbarossa episode has grown less important over the years, her own role becoming faded and hazy. But it seems that it changed her parents' life for good.

"The only reality is one's own past."

Which pessimist had said that? Emma could not remember, but she had to admit that it was true. In the silent night, her life was only recollections, her memory as clear and fluid as water. It spread out endlessly over an infinite area in which she was suspended.

Her bed, the bell by her hand, the gently billowing curtains, the sleeping Judith, the unseen objects that she had treasured for so long, the photograph of Bruno on her bedside table.

She was a butterfly on its last flight, flitting, fleeting.

Oscar Verschuur and Kate Dudok were so close that she could touch them.

Conversations with her mother almost always teetered on the brink of argument. Their words rarely converged, rarely alighted on common ground. What did they really know about each other? Had her mother ever wondered?

In 1939 Kate had gone to live in London. She and Oscar were scared of Germany and bought a house where they thought it would be safe. He had been transferred to Bern, and Kate found work in a London hospital. She lived instinctively, without a plan and without Oscar.

Kate's nomadic existence, which she continued after the war, with London as her base, foiled any attempts at reconciliation. For Michael and Thomas, their grandmother was something like a story, they saw her once or twice a year at most, more or less by chance.

Kate traveled mainly in Africa, where she knew and helped many people. Letters, the few she wrote, came from Élisabethville, Congo, where at least she had a postal address.

She had once sent a photograph of herself from there, with a black man and his wife and three children, all strangers to Emma. Kate had one of the children on her lap, the man was wearing a hat, his wife was smiling, the children were looking at Kate. Black idyll with white woman, a scene from Kate Verschuur's mysterious life. They were strange signals from a strange world. Feeling uncomfortable, Emma had stored the photograph away. There was a message encrypted within it that she preferred not to decipher. And she also felt a little envious, for you could see that her mother knew the children in the photograph better than she did her own grandchildren.

18

"Do you know where I was when your father died?"

One day, years later, Kate had, of course, told her anyway, even though Emma had never asked. The story lay at the bottom of her memory, a sunken tale in which her mother had revealed more about herself than ever before. Tonight, that story resurfaced.

Kate had taken a trip with a man called Matteous Tunga, along the River Congo, a thousand miles northwards toward Ethiopia. Matteous wanted to return to the jungle of his childhood. He had once been recruited as a soldier in an army that was going to liberate Ethiopia. Even before they got there, his platoon had walked into a trap and came under fire. His officer was seriously wounded and, when Matteous had picked him up and carried him out of the line of fire, he was himself shot in the back.

After a long search, he and Kate had found the scene of the ambush. Scene of the ambush, but also the site of a new beginning. By repeating his journey, Kate said, Matteous had wanted to exorcise his horror of the war, his disgust for the Belgian officers who commanded black battalions and marched them to face the Italian army, which was occupying Ethiopia.

After the ambush he had been transported to London, to a friend of the wounded Belgian, a surgeon at the Richmond Royal Hospital, where Kate worked. She had nursed him and helped him through his recovery.

Matteous had returned to the Congo in the middle of the war. He wanted to take back the life that had been stolen from him. Kate, his temporary pseudo-mother, did not expect to see him again. The sea crossing alone was very risky. Hoping against hope, she had given him twenty postcards addressed to her. He sent her all of them over five years. Every few months a postcard would drop through her letterbox, signed in a kind of hieroglyphics. And each time there were more words in English, written phonetically.

Kate knew the contents of the cards by heart. She had found her destination: Africa.

"What exactly do you mean by 'Africa,' Mother?"

Irritation in every syllable. Kate's answer is simple: "We've lost sight of Africa. We need to find it again. The people need our help."

These are bold phrases, rather empty, and yet Emma finds them moving. Her mother, the little bulldozer, is preparing to go into battle again. For five years she lived in a city under fire, and now that peace has broken out she is looking for another front. She has given her husband as much freedom as possible, even though they are still married, for the sake of what once was, and perhaps the love they once shared gives them some indefinable sense of comfort.

"What kind of man is this Matteous? And why did you go with him on his journey?"

Kate finds it hard to explain. It was the first time she had seen him again. For eleven years, she had thought about him every day. The journey was already mapped out, he left her no choice, his wife and children knew exactly who she was when she finally arrived, and that she and Matteous were going to make the journey together. A trip inland, into the dreaded past.

"He had to go back there. I didn't really understand it at first either. Why return to a place where you were shot? But he was determined, it was something he was going to do, no matter what, and I had to go with him. He'd got hold of an old army Jeep, a cat on wheels, we jumped from one pothole to the next. You don't get anywhere out there without that kind of vehicle. A week later, when we eventually found the spot where he so very nearly died, there was a gale blowing, as hot as a fire. The River Congo was close by, and there were a few clumps of bushes and trees scattered on a bare strip of land all the way to the jungle, which rose up like a wall. Matteous looked around. He seemed composed, and yet somehow absent. He was there, yes—but he wasn't. Then he showed me the route his platoon had taken, as precisely as if he had been there only the day before and his fellow soldiers were now resting somewhere beneath the trees.

"He told me what had happened that afternoon in early 1941, when the sun was already low in the sky. As they were looking for a place to spend the night, shots had been fired at the group from various directions.

"When Matteous told the story, he didn't look at me. Everything he said was filled with unfathomable grief and loss. For his fellow soldiers, for his own life. Then he began to talk about his mother. He had last seen her when he was a boy of seven, before she was taken away by a gang of thugs, so-called freedom fighters, who had just murdered his father.

"'Miss Kate'—he always calls me Miss Kate—'after I had taken my officer to safety, in those trees over there, I collapsed and fell to the ground. I hoped I'd never wake up again. Then I would go to my mother. But they rescued me, they moved me halfway around the world and when I woke, you were at my bedside. You were the one who got me through it all. Without you, I wouldn't be here and I wouldn't have a wife and children. Miss Kate, will you be the grandmother to my children?'"

Emma listens to her mother's voice, she listens in silence, with a respect she has never felt before. So that's why she looks as if she belongs in that picture Emma has hidden away: she *does* belong. Matteous took her mother to that remote spot to ask his surrogate mother to be his children's grandmother. A complicated way of doing things, perhaps an African custom, or maybe evidence of psychological insight: traveling back in time together to ask a question that would have sounded inappropriate at home.

"We got out of the Jeep and walked to the edge of the jungle, where there was less wind. And a little deeper into the trees you could hear the storm only high up above. That's where Matteous told me that the gunman who had got them had probably belonged to the same mob that had attacked his village. He'd realized that his mother was probably no longer alive, but this wasn't confirmed until after the war. Rumors travel fast in the Congo, but the truth moves slowly."

She thought about how she had never met Matteous. He was a part of her mother's life, which made him a part of her own.

Was he still alive somewhere, with his children and grandchildren? How old would he be? No, he must be long dead by now, people in Africa did not grow old, and she herself was already ninety-six. One more day, maybe a couple. It all depended on the team.

19

"It's the world that's old, not you."

A sentence blown in on the breeze, where did it come from, who had said it? Bruno?

Carl. Her birthday in Berlin, she had turned twenty-nine and had asked Carl if he thought she was old now. Twenty-nine, an incredible age, a pivotal point in an excited, agitated life. In a world that could end at any moment.

Berlin, 1941. Celebrating a birthday in a respectable suburb, dancing to forbidden music, getting dizzy on cheap wine and stories of hope.

Time was transparent. Judith slept on peacefully. After all those nights she had spent half-awake, she could not keep her eyes open on this last night.

"Simon, are you asleep? Could you not watch with me for just one hour?"

Another sentence drifting in from nowhere. Jesus in Gethsemane, the hero of Louis, the man she had debated with for a year about faith and the lack of it. All the way into his arms. Louis Terpstra, a temporary refuge. Whatever had possessed her to let things go so far? What did he see in her, and what on earth did she see in him?

Louis came to Rotterdam once a fortnight to teach a course in philosophy, theology and poetry. A man with crepe soles, cigar ash on his lapel, a wave in his hair, a faded raincoat, but with a voice you believed.

In the end his infatuation began to bother her, but even so he had managed to carry out a good deal of successful missionary work. Because Emma's fascination with Christ had remained, even when she no longer wanted to see Louis. "I believe, help my disbelief"—Psalms, the Song of Songs, the parables, miracles, those deadly pronouncements, each and every one had a sound that appealed to her.

Tonight, everything came within her reach. Lines of poetry, prose, fictional characters from the books she had read, with whom she was sometimes on more intimate terms than with her friends. Strange how the ghosts from a writer's head could come almost physically close to you. Including Jesus of Nazareth, a thirty-three-year-old man from Palestine, a teacher for Louis, and also for her, for as long as it lasted.

Bruno also believed that Jesus had been a miracle in world history, but for him Jesus was not the beginning and the end. Emma remembered, word for word, what Bruno had said when he came home one Sunday morning. Michael and Thomas were still young, she had not gone with him that day to the church where they occasionally listened to sermons.

He told her how the female pastor—it was a liberal church where they quoted more from world literature than from the Bible, and where women stood in the pulpit—had discussed the parable of the rich man. He had done all that Jesus said, followed all the Commandments, except for one thing: Jesus had told him to sell his belongings, give the money to the poor and to follow him. But he simply could not do it. "And he went away sad." That sentence had rankled with Bruno.

"Jesus let him go away sad, Emma. Leave aside the impossible command to sell everything you've built up in your life, it's cruel to allow a man like that, a better man than most, to go away sad. That's not right. What kind of Messiah makes such unrealistic demands?"

Emma had cheerfully replied that she could think of another gem from Jesus on the same subject: "It's easier for a camel to pass through the eye of a needle than for a rich man to enter the Kingdom of Heaven."

Bruno had started earning more at that point and had become a member of the board at cousin Chris' factory. Wealth beckoned, or at least poverty had been averted, and the Kingdom of Heaven placed at a safe distance.

Chris Dudok's factory was flourishing. Emma and Bruno also profited from that success, as the shares she had inherited from her mother increased in value every year. It was only after her mother's death, exactly seventeen years after Oscar's, that Emma had understood why she had been able to travel so easily and to help all those Africans. She had been rich. The Dudoks had been accumulating wealth for a century, they were people of independent means, and entrepreneurs to boot. Emma had never wondered how her mother was able to keep a flat in London and her father a house in Switzerland. And then there was that enormous house in Leeuwarden, where her grandparents had lived. She did not want to know, she had never been interested in money.

That was just as well, because in their street everyone was equal, they all had the same number of rooms, a balcony, a fireplace, a cellar and a bicycle shed. Wealth did not count. The cars out on the street did become bigger, though, as the years went by, and the bicycles had more gears.

Then the time came when the street's veterans moved to detached houses surrounded by gardens, some distance away, over the border, out into the world. One by one, they left until finally only Bruno and Emma remained, and Bruno was the only resident who had lived there throughout the war. The street had been a fortress where the residents were safe. It was an armor-plated group of friends who looked after one another's children, ate together, fell in love time and again, hid out at one another's houses when the Krauts made their raids, who shared the food that fell from the sky onto their flat roofs in '45, organized parties, children's birthdays, celebrations for Queen's Day. The street of their life, and the end would never come. But it did.

Now Emma was the only one left, her house was still just as it had been when she came here for the first time and Maarten had put his head around the balcony partition and said, "Welcome to the street, Emma!" Maarten and Maria, their neighbors and best friends, a gang of four until death did them part. First Bruno, then Maarten, then Maria and soon Emma herself.

Judith slept soundly through all of Emma's thoughts. It was pleasant, Emma listened to her breaths, and to the silences between. The sleeping girl was a great source of peace.

20

The factory's board meeting was always held in an upstairs room at De Reünie. Bruno was early, which was not like him. But he did not mind, as the empty club had a soothing effect. Light streamed into the room through the high windows, filtered by net curtains. Bridge tables stood ready and waiting for a competition that never seemed to end, the reading table gleamed, the barman was the only one around. The meeting would not begin for another hour.

The barman brought him tea.

"Mr. Dudok is already upstairs, Mr. Verweij."

Bruno stood up, took his tea and headed upstairs. Exactly as he'd later told Emma, who had listened to the story, pale and rigid.

"Huh, fancy you already being . . ." Then not another word.

Bruno, in the doorway, his hand on the doorknob, sees Chris sitting at the long conference table, head bowed, hands over his eyes, still in his coat and hat. He is crying, almost silently. Chris, all starch and stiff creases, as Bruno and Emma sometimes said to each other, a man who never made a fuss about anything, and who would be the last to reveal his emotions, is sitting there, overwhelmed by sadness, lost within himself. He jumps when he realizes someone is watching him.

"Bruno!"

In a few strides, Bruno is with him, taking him by the shoulders.

"She's dead. She was killed back then, in the bombing. I always thought as much, but I didn't know for certain. And now I do. She no longer exists. And I wish I didn't exist either."

Bruno lets him speak, asks no questions, even though he does not understand much of what Chris is saying, he just holds him.

The tears passed, but what Chris told Bruno remained with him forever.

Emma had not interrupted Bruno even once, but he must have noticed how she had listened, frozen, to his story. Her old life had suddenly returned, as a mirror image, in Chris' story she recognized her years with Carl.

Chris met her before the war, in Lübeck, where he had gone to work for a year. Her name was Julia. A German woman. She took everything he had always thought true and possible and turned it upside down. That one year, when he had been able to see her and to love her, had thrown him entirely off course. He wanted to shake off his existing commitments and not return home, all he wanted was to be with Julia, and to do whatever he could to get her out of that damned, doomed country. But she said no.

"Julia opposed the regime, Bruno, she was carrying out her own personal guerrilla war. She was completely independent, with such a clear conviction and her brother in a concentration camp. Kristallnacht changed everything. Julia forced me to leave the country as soon as possible, she said I'd be putting her in danger if I stayed. She didn't want to go with me, she had to take care of some friends and to try to get her brother released. She was determined, she said she loved me, but she wouldn't let me talk her round. She promised she would follow me, and I left. I was cowardly enough to leave. I've never felt at home anywhere since."

Emma suddenly had a clear recollection of how strangely Chris had reacted when he opened the door to her that first time, after she came back from Germany. For a split second he had seen Julia, that must have been it.

"Christ, Emma! For a moment I thought . . ."

Julia. Carl. Both of them German, both faithful to an unknown God, to an ingrained notion that you do not abandon a friend, or a brother, or a country. Better to die than to betray yourself. Emma knew all about that, the unbending seriousness, the steely courage, the unshakable morality that would not be seduced, not even by love.

Chris had struggled with it for another twenty years: Julia and his regrets and his powerlessness. Emma and Chris had become a kind of brother and sister. Over time, they had come to imagine that they really were siblings. Chris called Emma "sister," and she referred to him as "brother Chris." Cousins, brother and sister, what difference did it make? Their innocent fantasy was in keeping with their sense of kinship. They were strange allies, that was true, the cynic and the searcher, the childless arch-pessimist and the dedicated mother of two.

Dedicated, yes, she was certainly that. From the moment Michael was born, she wanted nothing more than to be with him, to look at him, to play with him and carry him around, to push him along through life. In a pram, on a sledge, on the front of a bicycle, on the tram into town and quickly back again. He who leaves his room will perish.

Emma became entirely and exclusively a mother, and she did not look back. She mothered Thomas, who came along a year after Michael, even more, if that were possible. No one needed to know what had happened in the country she came from. She would live, have children, and love fearlessly.

She had done all three, and here she was, exhausted, with one more night to go.

21

The shock at his suicide is overwhelming.

On the day before Chris' funeral, Emma enters his big, frozen house. She sits at the window overlooking the pond. They have sat there so often, Chris on one side of the long table, she on the other.

He never gave anything away. At most Emma noticed only that the sense of emptiness, every time she saw him, seemed to have grown larger, the loneliness stronger, the unspoken aversion to a soulless existence more intense. Emma always remained his sister, certainly. The incorrigibly optimistic mother, someone who goes to church, reads poems, knows the Bible, a sweet innocent knocking on the closed doors of his armored universe.

"I wish I didn't exist either" and "I've never felt at home anywhere since"—those two sentences echo in her mind. Sentences she had never forgotten. A warning? A veiled threat?

A prediction of his end—always feared, never acknowledged. So it had finally come to this. Van Dijk, Chris' left- and right-hand man, who drove him around, cooked, did the shopping for him, called her to pass on the unfathomable news, the world spun around her, she had to sit down, the telephone on her lap. The telephone, that venomous, elegant and seductive tool, bearer of tidings good and ill.

"I just wanted to let you know that . . . ," "Thank goodness I've got hold of you . . . ," "Sadly . . . ," "You'd better sit down . . ."

Carl, Rob, Oscar, Kate, Bruno, and now Chris: atomized in one telephone call. The same bell that rings for everyone, about everyone, news announced by a shattered voice or a composed one.

It is half past three in Chris' house of death, where Emma is sitting at the table. At home, school is finishing for the day, the bell usually drifts through the open windows toward her. She knows the scene so well, the throngs of bicycles and scooters, the boys and girls with rucksacks, pushing and shoving one another as they race outside. It makes her glad, every time she sees it. The world could end, disasters occur all over the world, but school empties with the heedlessness of a new-born baby. An explosion of happiness, children leaving a school. Free! Emma has watched it hundreds, thousands of times, the sounds hitting high against the walls of her house in this daily ritual. Often she opens her window for a little while, to let in the shouts and the laughter.

A clock in the hallway strikes four times. A smaller one on the window ledge mimics it. Even without its occupant, everything in the house retains its regularity: the fridge hums, the clocks tick, the barometer works, the garden sprinkler reacts to the weather, the lights go on automatically when it gets dark, the meters in the cupboard whir.

Emma feels the house moving inaudibly, breathing in and out, the daily routine. Chris is lying in a building at the crematorium. Van Dijk has avoided the house since he found his boss dead in the study. She collected the key from him and now she is just sitting there. How in God's name could anyone want to say goodbye to such a perfect view? A lawn beside an old pond, groups of trees with squirrels playing in them. Moorhens darting from lily pad to lily pad, fish popping to the surface every now and then. Crows high in the sky, rhododendrons, a sundial, a deck with wicker chairs, croquet hoops in the grass, the flagpole, an apple tree. A dome of tranquility: here lives a man who has inherited paradise.

But apparently not. It seems that in the end all this made no impression on him, nothing did. The ground became rock where nothing could grow.

Emma never spoke a word about what she had heard from Bruno about Julia. Chris did not even allude to the incident at any time. Old stories should be allowed to rest in peace, that is what she has always done.

Let the dead rest, and love the living.

Was it really because of Julia that Chris could see no way to go on? She can scarcely believe it. So he had been walking around with a dead woman for almost forty years, who had grown heavier and heavier, year after year after year.

She stands up, the room has windows on every side, the sun shines in on cupboards and tables, the dried flowers on top of the piano. The varnish gleams on the paintings, whisky glasses on a silver tray reflect the light. On the corner of a desk she sees a photograph frame lying face down, its stand in the air. Fallen over, a disruption of all that Van Dijk's hand has so strictly ordered and arranged.

Emma takes the frame, stands it upright and looks into her own face. It is an old photograph, taken when she was still staying with Chris and Imke. A lifetime ago. Chris had asked her to pose for him, he wanted to try out his new camera.

Julia, she must always have reminded him of Julia, from the day she returned from Germany. That was why he had photographed her.

Emma does not want to look any longer, and puts the photograph back down flat. Had Chris perhaps done the same, deliberately? As a gesture of farewell, apology for what he was going to do—you don't have to look, you can't see anything, you don't exist anymore, everything is dark.

Emma walks slowly around the room. She passes the piano on which no note was ever played, its sheaf of yellowing sheet music never used. Into the kitchen, down the hallway, up the stairs into the study and the bedroom. For a moment she wonders if she is allowed to walk around Chris' house like this, like a detective tracking his final movements, because that is what she is doing. She is walking in his footsteps, following the trail to the study where he swallowed his pills.

Nothing seems to have been touched, the room looks as if Chris might return at any minute to continue with whatever he was working on. On his desk are books and papers, an envelope with a piece of string tied around it, an old newspaper—a German one, she notices immediately—a fountain pen with its cap beside it, a few rubber bands and stamps. Work in progress, he has just been called away by Van Dijk, he will be back soon.

Emma hesitates, and then sits down at the desk. Van Dijk told her that he had found Mr. Dudok close to his desk.

"The door was half open, Mrs. Verweij, he was lying with one hand through the doorway." Details she does not want to know.

And on the desk there had been a bowl with remnants of porridge, a napkin on one side and a silver spoon on the other. Refinement to the bitter end.

The bowl has been removed, of course. She can still just about see the mark it has left on the thin film of dust on the desk, a scrap of evidence. The newspaper is a local one from Lübeck, she sees, from 1942, the year of the bombing—of the bombs all around her in Berlin, with Carl holding her tight.

Dear Chris, stupid, lonely, loyal Chris, what were you looking for in that newspaper? You had already known for so long. I'll find it for you: Julia Bender, died March 28, 1942.

On Palm Sunday, the day of Jesus of Nazareth's entry into Jerusalem. Louis had once given an excellent sermon on the subject. One week on the shoulders of the people, as hero and savior, the kingdom close at hand, the next week carrying a huge wooden cross through the streets, with the people splitting their sides.

Julia Bender in a burning house, it is an image that is not hard to imagine. No one who was sleeping in the center of Lübeck escaped. The British later spoke of a precision-bombing attack. Emma had long been familiar with the term, she had seen the bombs falling so often, although they always seemed to be dropped at random. But Chris had despised the British for it. Even though he dressed like an English gentleman of leisure, and would rather read English books than Dutch ones, the way they had killed people, attacking in the middle of the night like thieves and destroying historic cities, Dresden, Lübeck, Weimar—he thought these were Nazi methods. Emma had once heard him fulminating against British crimes, without mentioning Julia, and even then she had been surprised by his cynical view of the war.

Julia Bender, a name on that night's list of victims. Only those few sentences that Bruno had heard about her and passed on to Emma, that was all that remained of her. A handful of words and an entry in an index of the dead.

Emma sits at Chris' desk, her hands on the green blotter, and automatically screws the cap onto the fountain pen. Then she spots an open book. A sheet of paper is sticking out from under it at an angle. She looks at what Chris was reading. Schopenhauer: "Fate shuffles the cards, and we play."

Chris' favorite writer, a great thinker about the futility of everything and everyone. That book alone is a farewell, she realizes. No long letters with explanations, no apologies or blame, no dramatic words. An open book, a subtle handshake.

As she picks up the book, the whole sheet of paper becomes visible. There are two lines on it, in Chris' precise and precious handwriting. Emma knows the lines by heart, she does not even need to read them, she knows they are by Rilke, *their* poet. They did not agree about many things, always engaged in a kind of loving battle, but when it came to Rilke, there was no dispute.

Wer jetzt kein Haus hat, baut sich keines mehr. Wer jetzt allein ist, wird es lange bleiben.

Whoever has no house now will never build one, whoever is alone now will remain so for a long time.

A will after all, one last thought that he had written down for her, the last meal already prepared.

Chris, cousin, brother, companion in adversity, knight in shining armor, her favorite sparring partner. Now she is the one who is alone and will remain so for a long time. She is sixty-seven, not even old, all things considered.

Emma replaces the sheet of paper, even though she knows it is meant for her, the letter with no addressee. She does not want to disturb the order—or rather, disorder—of the desk. Everything must remain as it was, like evidence for a court, a dossier of helplessness.

How old was Chris? Seventy-two. He looked sixty, back like a ramrod, but no purpose in life. What a dreadful deed, and yet what incredible courage.

Wer jetzt allein ist, yes, that was right, alone, that was what she was now, no doubt about it.

Four years before Chris, it had been Bruno who had left her behind and he, too, had wasted few words.

"Call Michael and Thomas," he had said in the ambulance.

Bruno, her quiet husband, sick, caring, sporty, addicted to cigarettes, the beloved father. And then he had died, as they raced to the hospital at top speed.

All she had been able to do was hold his hand, look at his damaged fingernails, see how gray his hair was, how ashen his face, his parted lips. His cardigan and shirt were torn open, the watch on his wrist twisted around, its strap broken. A man was pounding on his chest, she heard the sound of his ribs cracking. The neon lights in that claustrophobic space, the paramedic's sweat, the siren's wails.

"I'm losing him, I'm losing him," the medic had mumbled, more to himself than to her.

22

"Bruno!"

The nurse beside her was instantly awake.

"Do you need some help, Mrs. Verweij?"

"No, I don't believe so. Did you think I said something?"

"I heard you say 'Bruno.'"

"I need to call Michael and Thomas, Judith."

"You already phoned them, yesterday evening. Thomas is on his way."

"And Michael?"

"I'm sure he's coming too. He's not very well, remember?"

"What time is it, Judith?"

"Four o'clock, it'll be a while before it gets light. Try to get some more sleep, it'll do you good."

The lamb, the dear little lamb, she meant it so sincerely: "It'll do you good."

The light would come, without a doubt. The sun would shine upon her room, her balcony, the objects in her house. Suddenly she felt amazed at the existence of light, something that made it possible to see. How many times had she wandered around her flat at night when she was unable to sleep? Fumbling to open the curtains, which she always shut every night, as if the war were not over. An old habit from Berlin.

On some snowy nights, a few streetlights still shining, not a soul around, she would watch, the world all to herself, as the snow fell, calm and steady. Layer by layer, it changed the view, as the street narrowed and became a freshly made bed. Snow was just about the simplest form of happiness, snow was her father in Switzerland, the skating trips in Friesland, going out with Bruno and Michael and Thomas through the white streets.

In the Black Forest, the snow falls in huge quantities. It is December 1944 and Emma is living with the Rupert family, the father is a brother of Elka Wapenaar's, in Korntal, a village like an open-air museum. Houses in delicate shades, a square with a pub, a school and a church. And, all around, farmland, corn fields, spruce woods, cows and horses, pigs and goats.

It is indecently peaceful, the war seems far away. But the tranquility is deceptive, as there are hardly any young men around, just children and women and old men. A village without muscle, nice and quiet. The Wapenaars managed to get Emma onto a train, which, after more than two days, had come to a halt at a godforsaken station on the edge of the Black Forest. Away from Berlin, city of murderers, where the zoo is open as usual, and the football matches go on and the films still play in the cinemas. It turned her stomach.

Snow just before Christmas, she would have taken a sledge out onto the street before, but Emma cannot afford to think about before. The memory is more painful than hunger and cold. In the village the old men talk about the Ardennes, where their grandsons have been sent, in one last all-out effort against the enemy. It would work, it had to work. This is the offensive they have been hoping for. The women know better, they milk the cows, slaughter their last pigs and wait.

Emma is tolerated. She is an outsider, and people in the village suspect she was the wife of a traitor, the kind that wanted to murder the Führer. But Rupert is a decent man, they respect him, and he has said that Emma is part of the family and that they have to treat her decently.

The months at the Ruperts seem to last forever, first the autumn, then a harsher winter than any she can remember. When Christmas comes in Korntal, the Ruperts are the only family in the village who do not go to church. Not because they do not want to, but because there is an idiot in the pulpit, a full-blown Nazi. Emma goes anyway, on her own, leaving the Ruperts confused.

December 24, Christmas Eve, *Heiliger Abend*, the snow refuses to let up. A female choir that they have scraped together is singing as she comes in and finds a place in one of the rear pews. Emma has never been inside the church before. A few candles are burning in the almost-dark space, but it is bare and damp. The windows are covered with black paper. Dusty bags containing songbooks hang at intervals along the benches. And there are brass plaques screwed onto the backs of the pews. Everyone appears to have their own seat. She recognizes the names of some of the villagers, the baker and the vet. His place was at the back, of course, he had to be able to slip away if needed.

Emma braces herself for what is to come. She could not bear it in her little room, she had to get out, and she did not care where to. So she automatically joined the people who were heading to church. Something different for a change, a little time away from her doom-laden thoughts.

Church, she has scarcely a notion of what it means, she has been maybe once or twice, with her grandmother on Christmas Eve, in Leeuwarden, aeons ago in an age of fairy tales.

A man steps out of a side door and walks to the front. He is wearing an ordinary smart suit, presumably the one he wore to get married, which only comes out of the wardrobe on special occasions. Emma recognizes him, it is the vet. He climbs into the pulpit and says calmly that the pastor will not be coming, he has been called up to fight in the Ardennes. No one reacts. Then this rustic man, who has the good fortune to be over fifty and indispensable, raises his hand, as if to call a halt to something that cannot be seen.

"Peace be with you."

Emma looks around. Every head she sees is bowed and silent. This man is asking the impossible, but they listen with wondrous intent.

Packed in together, their names in brass, they sit there, worn to the bone, their sons and grandsons dead or who knows where, all of them impoverished, afraid and without hope.

This is how people are sitting all over Germany now, thinks Emma, in blind devotion. The windows blacked out, the candles lit.

The vet reads the story of the Nativity, as told by Luke, another medical man. A primitive account of a child born in a stable, but the story captivates her. To a vet, a birth in a stable is nothing special. The perfect setting, nice and warm.

The rural accent and the steady tones of the stand-in pastor's voice are so pleasant that Emma forgets time and place. As long as he is reading, talking, as long as the choir sings those age-old songs with their unintelligible words in archaic German, she forgets the war. She does not think about anything else, not Carl, not her parents, not herself.

Christmas in the Black Forest, in a dilapidated church on a hill not all that far from liberated France. Pseudo-mysticism, perhaps, but the voice of the veterinary surgeon and the hoarse choir of women and the draft that almost blows out the candles and the squeaking and wheezing of the little organ above her head—it is almost enough to make her believe. Peace be with you. If only that were possible, *bitte*.

The vet prays, the people around Emma mumble along. That a kingdom might come, and bread, and trespasses be forgiven and that they themselves might forgive those who trespass against them.

Such warm and friendly people. Murmuring. The sounds of an unknown lament, a flurry of words she can barely make out, led by the man in the pulpit. Helmut Wachter is his name, and he watches over them all.

23

Four o'clock, Judith had said. The end of the graveyard shift, the deepest moments of the night were over. It would soon be light, and Tuesday. Thomas would take matters in hand, final round, kingdom come.

Emma listened to see if the nurse had fallen back to sleep. Yes, she could hear the soft, regular breathing, the coast was clear. Centimeter by centimeter, she moved to one side of the bed, took hold of the sticks that were leaning against it and, trembling with the effort, she slipped silently out of her bedroom, pausing every so often to listen. A light was on in the hallway. The door to the living room was open, her chair was by the window, untouched.

As tired as if she had been walking for a day, Emma reached her lookout post.

"System, friend who takes everything from me, and soon the rest of my time—I feel like a stranger everywhere, except for in eternity."

The lines of poetry returned to her, like homing pigeons to their coop. They were still there, the pigeons across the way. The old pigeon man was dead, but he must have passed on his hobby to his son, as the creatures continued to fly their rounds every evening, and a man high up on the roof put his hand in the air and whistled.

His father had been waving at his birds in the same way when Bruno had asked her to stay.

"I feel like a stranger everywhere, except for in eternity." Every day she repeated that sentence. Words could not come closer to what she was experiencing. They coincided perfectly with the sense of dissolution in her body as she was lifted up, paper thin, to become a memory.

Emma hoped Judith would not wake up yet. She wanted to wait for the light here, like this, in her chair, to sit through the night, or what was left of it.

The nurse had said it would be May in two days' time and that she was looking forward to it. Emma had not responded. She liked May, but she would always have preferred to skip the first week. Remembrance Day, the commemoration of the dead, liberation, thoughts of Carl on a butcher's hook, Adam before a screaming judge, Emma on the run. Images she had struggled to suppress.

But it always proved difficult on those two days, with Bruno participating enthusiastically in the events of commemoration and celebration on May 4 and 5. He hung the flag out of the side window, at half mast, or fastened it to the balcony facing the street, glaring at the drivers who did not pull over for the minute's silence at eight o'clock. Even though he had not in fact lost anyone during the war. On the second day, they went out early, Michael and Thomas wearing orange hats, the flag raised high in the school playground, a lantern procession through the neighborhood. Bruno was in his element.

He seemed to have been liberated, but Emma sometimes wondered if that was really the case. Over time, his skin complaint had worsened, and the local chemist became a wholesale supplier of an endlessly changing list of medication. Experimental treatments, weeks in hospital, year after year.

The after-effects of that wartime winter of starvation, was the diagnosis. But was that true? Bruno had never said much about starvation. In fact, he had remained silent about that last year of the war.

Emma now knew why. Maria, who had become her best friend, had told her. By then, Bruno had been dead for about a year.

Emma and Maria were walking by the lake on a path close to the water, past tall reeds and paddling ducks. Not far from the shore were a few little islands. Crumbled away from the land, and overgrown with bushes and small trees. Large enough for a secret rendezvous, if you had a boat.

"That was our island." Maria points out the green strip of land in the water.

When Emma asks who she means by "our," she says: "Bruno's and mine."

"You and Bruno?"

"But surely you knew!"

Emma shakes her head. Maria grips her arm and steers her to one of the benches beside the path.

"In the war. It didn't last any longer than a year, maybe eighteen months. Two years at most."

That probably means twice as long, throughout the war, thinks Emma, but she does not say so.

Maria's story is fragmented, full of gaps and contradictions, it is a story awash with embarrassment and old desire. Maria does now what Bruno never wanted to do: she talks about the war years in their street, the oasis they designed and dreamed up themselves, their bastion of self-confidence, humor, love and recklessness. There were raids and hunger there too, they came from outside, they were unavoidable. And there was also fear, and a stillborn child, and parents who died, and a brother who was executed by the Germans.

"Most of us were between twenty-five and thirty-five, about twenty young families, a few elderly people, two female friends who lived together, and one friendly member of the National Socialist Movement, who never hurt anyone but himself. We lived in a street that was two hundred meters long at most, with broad pavements, a few streetlights, six young trees. The street was our life. Looking back, it was madness to be so happy in those years, a little criminal, in fact. Bruno was the only man without a wife, but that didn't seem to be a problem for him. Quite the opposite, I'd say."

"How did it begin between the two of you, Maria?"

It had been when they were sailing. Bruno sailed until late in the autumn. And when everyone else had already prepared their boats for winter, he was often still out on the lake. One day in November, when it was sunny and unusually warm, he had asked Maria to go with him. At parties in the street they had often spoken to each other, he saw her, and she saw him, it was effortless, they danced together, they had never danced so much as during the war.

"I had the children, and Maarten—we only met occasionally, it was an air-raid-shelter kind of love, far from the real world, there was never any suggestion that we would ever get together. But it gave my days an extra sparkle, and his too. And then there came a point when we had to choose, people in the street were becoming suspicious, someone warned me that we'd been seen on the island."

Once again she points at that strip of land, which seems little more than a large clump of soil with a few bushes on it, and then is silent for a while.

When Maria continues, Emma has stopped listening, she is wandering through Bruno's life. He was lonely and gentle. She loved him without looking back. Maria's story does not shock her, not at all, in fact. She is glad that he was not alone in those dark years.

It had ended in the summer of '44, is that what Maria said?

Bruno and Maria had been to their island for the last time, the reeds were head-height, they had agreed on a retreat to their homes, with feelings of emptiness and of circumstances beyond their control. Is that how it had happened?

Maria just keeps talking, as if the truth is pursuing her. She wants to shake off this story, to tell what cannot be told. But Emma hears something else, she sees something else, and suddenly she thinks she understands what happened. And, strangely, that does not shock her either.

"When did it begin again, Maria?"

A part of Bruno had always remained in the shadows for her, it seemed to be something he could not comprehend himself. Emma had sometimes found him in tears. She can picture him in the dim light, at that round antique table of his father's, his hand on the arm of the chair, a cigarette between his dark-yellow fingertips. Far away, in some foxhole in unknown territory.

Yet Maria's answer still takes her by surprise.

"For me, it never stopped. I let go of Bruno back then, that summer. But I missed him constantly. After he met you, he treated me like his little sister, with a stubborn sense of loyalty. I often visited our island again in my mind, but never in reality."

A stubborn sense of loyalty? More like desperate perhaps. They're unfortunately chosen words, although Maria probably doesn't realize.

Emma thinks about Bruno in his little bunker, lost in silence. Whenever it happened, she had waited, she was better at waiting than anyone she knew.

Her friendship with Maria had only grown closer after this "confession."

24

Morning came. Emma saw the first cars going by on Oudedijk, headlights on, full speed ahead into the city. She slowly turned her bracelet, the smooth silver band with the small silver clasp, which she had never taken off since the day she received it from Maria.

"Bruno once gave it to me. I never dared to wear it. It's for you."

That had been shortly after her confession. Bruno had been dead for thirty-three years now. Emma had worn the bracelet all that time, only removing it briefly to clean it.

Thirty-three years alone, sixty-two years in the street. Counting up the years, it made her head spin. So many years with Carl, so many with Bruno, so many without. Maria was no longer alive either.

Emma was not entirely certain that Maria had answered truthfully when she had asked when it had started again. It had sounded convincing, but looking back it had seemed too practiced, an answer learned by heart. Particularly the part about the "stubborn sense of loyalty," which seemed almost to emphasize the *lack* of loyalty. In retrospect.

Even looking back, though, and with the pain of Bruno's death still palpable and all-pervading, Emma had felt neither anger nor jealousy. She did not want to go digging into secrets that Maria and Bruno might have, it would only put her friendship with Maria at risk. Anyone who wishes to uncover secrets of that kind, she decided, has never loved.

Somewhere a church bell struck five. It must be the Koninginnekerk—no, that had been torn down years ago, after a hard-fought battle between two camps of believers. A hole in the neighborhood, now filled with new houses, but the hours had continued to ring in people's memories for years.

Emma listened out for Judith. It would not be long before she discovered she was gone. But there was just the silence of the rooms around her.

If Thomas was going to arrive in time, he would need to be getting up now. It was a morning's journey from Hamburg to Rotterdam. He had said eleven o'clock, that was when he would arrive. She still found it remarkable that he had gone to live in Clarita's city. He felt at home there, he claimed. He was no doubt influenced by his father. After every trip, Bruno talked about how the young Germans had to bear the burden of their parents' past, and how they were dealing with the literal and figurative heaps of rubble.

Like the center of Rotterdam, Hamburg had been flattened by bombs. The Koninginnekerk over and over again, a vast number of gaps, a map of the soul that was now beyond comprehension: memory had become a labyrinth in which nothing was in the same place as before and all directions were lost.

Thomas. And Michael, her first-born, who was so sick that Emma could hardly bear to look. Her greatest fear was that his condition would worsen. Her proud son and yet, from the very beginning, her problem child. Emma had never entirely understood him, even though they were so alike in many ways. As a young boy Michael had been unmanageable, she had even sent him to stay with a cousin for a while, to cool down.

He had been four years old and yet was already conscious of this rejection. Sent away, farmed out, abandoned in an unfamiliar household. Emma had felt just the same when her parents had left her with her grandparents in Leeuwarden. The mirror image of an old wound. How strange that everything appeared to repeat itself, different in the details but essentially the same.

And the worst memory. One she would not manage to escape tonight.

25

How old had he been? Fifteen, sixteen, she cannot remember. But that does not matter, it is now.

Emma beats Michael. Hard, wherever she can hit him, in a wordless, ice-cold fury. He fends her off as best as he can. Stunned by the attack, which he did not see coming.

It is over before he realizes what is happening. Half a minute, which resounds for a lifetime.

Yes, he was sixteen, and he had said something about Carl, something he had read or heard somewhere. He had said it in a slightly provocative way, that was true, but he sounded more surprised than anything, just an observation about something that, as far as he was concerned, had been over for a long time, something from the war.

That she had been married to a traitor.

He was sixteen and rebelling against everyone and everything. Her response was to hit out, to make a stand against ignorance. She hit them apart forever. Maybe Michael, too, felt like a stranger everywhere, with his tentative footsteps, his life in the interrogative form. Emma had never been able to make up for that half minute, the arm he raised to defend himself had never been lowered.

Emma had pushed her unbearable regret and guilt into the realm where Carl resided, ever present, always emerging at the wrong moment. But recently her guilt had become so strong that she wondered if it was that brief fight that had triggered Michael's illness, a fire that did not break out until much later. It was possible—how much do we really know? At times she was certain.

Later, she had heard from Clarita von Trott that people had looked down on her, too, because of Adam, a traitor in the eyes of some of his compatriots, the man who had stood in court and viciously lashed out at the criminal regime and its lying henchmen.

"Nurse!"

The ambulance door is pulled open, two nurses take hold of the trolley and push it along a brightly lit corridor. One connects the oxygen, the other holds the nose mask, but she stumbles, the plastic mask slips, Bruno's head lolls. The operating theater in neon light, frosted-glass doors automatically opening and closing.

"Nurse, I have to help him!"

But they do not let Emma in. The door closes in her face. Now she is huddled in a waiting room next to the operating theater. Muffled sounds come through the walls. Bruno is lying in there, or whatever is left of him. She needs to let Maria and Maarten know. And did she blow out the candles at home?

Someone comes in silently. Emma sees a shadow, she looks up. It is Michael.

Almost as pale as Bruno, she thinks.

He nods toward the operating theater, says nothing. And then, softly: "Thomas is on his way, he'll be here in an hour."

Bruno, Bruno, don't leave me, it's too soon, there's still so much for us to do, to talk about.

The sounds have stopped, all is quiet. Then the door of the operating theater opens gently, as if to avoid disturbing the dead person lying there on the table.

The lights go out, the doctor's coat comes off, someone clears their throat. Michael's hand on her bowed head.

Thomas was going to catch the eight-thirty flight. Emma had worked out that he could be there by half past ten, if everything went smoothly. A weekday, Tuesday, sunrise at ten past six. End of April, spring, with summer on the way. But the sedation team would not let it come to that, Emma predicted contentedly.

Thomas and Michael. The names came up fairly often in sermons. Michael, the archangel, protector of the dying, and Thomas, who had to see before he believed. Louis had once pointed out the meanings to her and asked if she had chosen them for that reason.

No, she and Bruno had leafed through the Bible, so many parents' favorite book of names, it had been the sound alone, there was nothing else behind it. But now it seemed to Emma as if her sons' names had a deep significance. Michael, patron saint of the dying—who came up with such things? When Bruno died, Michael had stood in the waiting room at the hospital, silent and focused. He had protected her. And today Thomas would see, and he would have to believe. He would stand by his mother, his hand in hers.

26

What was it that her mother had said?

"I thought you always discussed everything, had no secrets from each other." It was about her father, "Oscar," as she had come to call him after his death. Her mother had remained "Mother," a description with little emotion attached. She had been her mother, of course, but there had been little resemblance, everyone said Emma was the spitting image of her father. There was nothing Dudok about her.

She had difficulty picturing her mother's face. Weathered skin, brown age marks, almost white hair, blue veins like cords on her hands. An African magician. She had rolled in and out of Emma's life, without making a fuss, leaving little behind. Kate Dudok, Kate Verschuur, her mother, names of a stranger, someone who had not made herself known to her. With a grave on the other side of the world, near Élisabethville.

And yet she was with her, too, Emma could not avoid her, she kept turning up tonight. This time with her remark about Oscar and their secrets. That was a misunderstanding, Oscar had told her as little as her mother, if not less. But, strangely enough, what her father had kept hidden from her was no longer a problem now—what annoyed her was what her mother had concealed or half-concealed. Or just casually revealed, such as the existence of Lara van Oosten, a subject that Oscar had so deliberately avoided.

Switzerland is a mirage, a country that floats some way above the ground, untouched, untouchable, pampered, a land like a rumor.

It is the late 1960s and Emma is driving alone through Switzerland. Bruno's Citroën D.S. sways along the road, a waterbed on wheels and the ideal car for the mountains. Emma traveled there every year, summer and winter, it went without saying. It was an ingrained habit, she went there with her parents even before the war, and then with Bruno and the children. Via Belgium and France, of course.

She breaks the journey in Bern for a small pilgrimage. Bern is the city where Oscar had spent the war. It feels like a solemn commemoration, her own May 4 in the autumn.

It is the beginning of November, a month when almost all the hotels in the mountains are closed. The sun provides little warmth, there is no snow on the ground as yet, it is quiet and empty, so close to the beginning of the tourist season.

Emma knows of one hotel that remains open all year round: Hotel Jungfrau. Where you can lie in bed and listen to the trains arriving and leaving on the cogwheel railway, model trains at a small station, spectral apparitions at a high altitude in the November mist.

She leaves the car in Lauterbrunnen and takes the train up the mountain to Hotel Jungfrau. A married couple sit a few seats away, surrounded by suitcases. The woman is wearing an elegant fur hat and a long black coat. The man is gray, but still looks young. As they get out, he holds out his hand to support her, the kind of gesture that means more than can be seen.

The hotel has sent porters for the luggage. Emma walks slowly up the steep path to the entrance. A dense mist has enveloped the outside dining areas, the light from the hotel windows barely penetrating it. Five o'clock, it is already getting dark, the fire in the lobby is lit. Emma writes her name in the guestbook. Everything is just right, Swiss precision ensuring everything and everyone is as advertised. The world here is a perfect diorama, a dance party.

For the first time in ages she is alone. Bruno, Michael and Thomas have their own business to attend to: work, study, a conference in Krefeld. Emma is concerned about Bruno, but that is a constant. His illness ebbs and flows, but always returns. He is smoking two packets of cigarettes a day now, his index and middle finger are stained by the nicotine, it cannot be good. But he still skates long distances with ease and beats his sons at tennis, "so everything's perfectly fine, Emma. No need to worry!"

"Excuse me. I'm sorry, but could I ask you something? Did you once live in Berlin?"

The woman from the train is standing at her table, without the fur hat and long coat now, but still just as elegant. A woman of around sixty, maybe a little older, it is hard to tell. Her question is so tentative that Emma is not even startled or puzzled by the fact that she is speaking Dutch.

It is a question she is never asked, or rather, one that she knows how to avoid. But even so, she is prepared. A couple of guests sit by the fire, talking quietly, a waiter brings glasses of beer, the hotel owner talks to newcomers, candles are lit in the dining room. Upholstered happiness, a burst of wealth.

Soon the pianist will start playing songs of yesteryear, the lid of the piano is already up.

With the same cautious tones as the woman, Emma replies: "Did we ever meet in Berlin? I'm sorry, I don't remember."

"No, we don't know each other, but I saw your name in the guestbook. You *are* Emma Verweij-Verschuur, aren't you? We signed in after you and I couldn't help reading your name. I once knew an Oscar Verschuur. He had a daughter in Berlin, she was called Emma and, well, to be honest, you look a lot like him. Please excuse my curiosity, it would be such a coincidence if it were you."

"Oscar Verschuur was my father."

Emma stands up as she says it, automatically shakes the woman's hand.

"Yes, I'm Emma. Would you mind telling me your name?"

"Lara van Oosten, at least it used to be. It's O'Brien now."

It is her. How is it possible that they are staying at the very same hotel?

Emma quickly sits down again. Lara van Oosten automatically takes a chair and slides it next to Emma's. At that moment the pianist begins his medley, good cheer all around, it is busy, nearly all the rooms are occupied. This hotel is a gathering place for those who love the empty mountains.

Strangely, Emma feels caught out, or more than that: guilty. Guilt is a misconceived form of responsibility, she reasons to herself. How idiotic to feel guilty for sitting with the woman her father loved.

Guilt, compassion and the wish to find out more fight for the upper hand. Emma's only option is silence. The woman briefly touches her hand, an apology. She does not speak either.

This silence is a kind of truce, they are unintentional allies, they know nothing about each other. Words are still absent, sentences, questions, the truth, all deferred. Fog at the windows, fire in the hearth, laughter drifts through from the kitchen, a barman shouts something.

"He died a long time ago, but you probably know that," Emma says at last.

The woman nods, yes, she knows. Her husband, an Irish diplomat, had told her.

"All the diplomats in Europe knew your father. They were devastated to hear of his death."

"What about you?"

Lara looks past Emma at her husband, who is standing nearby, waiting by the dining room. Many of the residents are already sitting down to dinner.

"My husband's waiting for me. Would you mind if we continued our conversation after dinner?"

"Is it that difficult?"

"I can't think straight right now. I hadn't imagined I'd ever meet you. I'd be happy to talk later, though."

She's still beautiful, thinks Emma as she watches Lara walk away. How stunning she must have been thirty years ago. Her father had certainly not been lacking in taste, lacking in morals perhaps, although Emma's opinions on such subjects have changed.

After dinner, Emma and Lara sit, familiar strangers, on a sofa by the fireplace. Old questions, new answers, a chance conversation, on a lost evening in November, in the Berner Oberland.

"Operation Barbarossa . . . Oscar knew the date of the invasion and I was under the naïve impression that tens of thousands of Russians might be saved if he warned the Allies. I did him a grave injustice, though. He was sure they would arrest you and have you executed. Those were his exact words, and

I didn't want to know, I thought him cowardly. I couldn't put myself in the position of a man with a daughter. I simply didn't believe the Allies would give him the brush-off, that they wouldn't believe him, as he insisted. He was right, of course, and I never forgave myself for letting him go away so very sad."

Letting him go away sad?

"But weren't you his lover for years? I thought he still saw you often, even after the war. Is that not right?"

Lara shakes her head.

"After June 19, 1941, at one thirty in the afternoon, we never met up again. We knew each other for four months and yes, we were lovers, I don't find it easy to say that to you, but that's how it was. He remained the focus of my life for years. I never spoke to him again, though. I saw him once, but he didn't see me. Six months after we ended the affair, I had to visit Bern. It was getting dark and it was snowing. I was walking across the square in front of the station with an umbrella in my hand when I saw him deep in conversation with another man. He didn't notice me, he was out without a hat or umbrella, the collar of his coat was turned up. They were gone before I knew it."

She stops speaking. Emma can see that the woman with whom she is having such an intimate conversation is unable to speak another word. As if she has only just heard what she is saying and has realized that she is talking to the daughter of the man she had come to love in such a short period of time.

Emma sits beside her, feeling somewhat lost and lonely. So her mother had only been speculating. Oscar had not led the double life that she had spoken about so casually.

Then she tells Lara about her years in Berlin, how she had cursed her father when he had not got in touch and had apparently done nothing with the news she had given him in Geneva. She had burdened him with Carl's secret, that the Germans were going to invade Russia on June 22 of that year. Of course she had been overflowing with the terrible possibility of an invasion, and of course she thought Oscar should know, maybe he could warn someone. But afterward she had blamed herself for involving him. Such childish behavior, calling in your father, making yourself the center of his attention. She should have taken immediate action herself and done something with the information.

Lara does not interrupt Emma even for a moment. Who knows, thinks Emma, maybe she can hear the sound of Oscar's voice. Then a log rolls off the carefully built fire, but even before it can land on the parquet floor, Emma has snatched a poker and pushed it back into the hearth, fast, nimble. Smiling, she holds up the poker. Victory. A waiter dashes over, asks what he can do for them. He must have thought Emma was trying to summon him to place an order.

"Oh, no, I wasn't calling you over, but now that you're here, I think we might well like to order something. Don't you, Mrs. O'Brien?"

"I do hope you'll call me Lara, and yes, a whisky, please. No ice."

Emma has an Irish coffee.

"Do you live in Switzerland, Lara?"

"No, I left during the war, got a job in Ireland. Better a neutral Ireland, I thought, than a neutral Switzerland. But it was probably more to escape your father."

How long has Oscar been dead now? More than fifteen years. With all the hundreds of deaths in that disastrous year of flooding, it was easy to be buried unnoticed. Who would pay attention to a mysterious diplomat being committed to the earth in Driehuis-Westerveld? A few stalwarts, a handful of relatives, a war comrade or two, most had already passed away.

Emma realizes that she has spoken freely about Carl, without hesitation. As if there were no Bruno, as if everything were as it once was. She and Carl in Geneva, in Berlin, in the all-encompassing grasp of the war and yet still in each other's arms, living from day to day.

"I've been here often since '41, Emma, at this hotel, I mean. It's incredible that we didn't meet sooner. We could easily have walked past each other, in the village or here. As soon as the war ended, I started coming here to ski almost every year, and we generally stay at this hotel."

"Hotel Jungfrau? We've taken holidays in Wengen for as long as I can remember, and this hotel was the ideal place for afternoon tea after skiing. I can't tell you how many times I've sat out on the terrace with my parents, and then later with my husband and children."

Lara says nothing, then everything.

"The first time Oscar saw me was here, at one of the tables outside. We met down in the village the next day, at Café Eiger. It didn't stop snowing, and that kept us inside the café all day. I don't know why or how it happened, but our lives suddenly slid together, out of nowhere. It was love, entirely unexpected, and a love that neither of us was looking for. The snow just went on falling. And, as lightly as snow falls, so mysterious and soft, that's how it happened between us. One day, and then four months, almost enough for a lifetime."

Emma recognizes what she hears.

27

The first patches of light on the houses spread slowly upward and downward. A few birds tentatively begin to whistle, a surprised sound—for anyone who listened. Emma heard them, for years now she had fed the tits, sparrows, finches and pigeons on a small shelf just outside the window, with a view of Oudedijk. Her own little nature table, nuts, pieces of crust that she carefully cut to beak size.

It was six o'clock, lines 16 and 17 were already running down Oudedijk, and some early cyclists were on their way to the center, briefcases on their racks.

Bruno had once told her that, in November 1944, all the men between seventeen and forty had been called up to work in Germany. Everyone in the street had received the order in the post. They were told to stand in front of their houses and then march together to the station.

In their street, no one had stood ready and waiting, but hundreds went marching along Oudedijk with suitcases and kitbags. A grim procession, at six in the morning. They were boys who had nowhere to hide, boys whose parents said, "Go on, it won't be as bad as you think," boys who wanted to go,

for whom anything was better than sitting around at home.
How many had made it through unscathed? Probably not one.
Rotterdam had mobilized more than fifty thousand men. Fifty
thousand, the biggest raid in Europe, one last convulsion. Now
almost forgotten.

Bruno and the men from the street, together with a few
other local lads, had spent a number of days in the basement
of the huge school building across the way. It was a poor hiding
place, fifty of them in coalholes, there was singing and shouting, someone had waved a pistol. More overconfident than
underground. Bruno thought it was a miracle that the Krauts
had not searched the school.

After that raid he stopped showing up at the office. The hunger set in, along with the cold. Maria was out of reach now, they
must have been lonely months. The street at its lowest point, he
had once let slip.

How many times had she and Bruno stood on the flat roof
of their building, looking out over the world, over the Rotterdam that he was helping to rebuild? And meanwhile he was
destroying himself. Smoking, endless unhealthy dinners, in
the car, out of the car, traveling, meetings, more meetings.
That was how he had died, as unexpectedly as he had come:
with an invitation to dance.

A ritual dance as it later turned out, a promise. A love in
peacetime.

That last winter of the war, the coldest, in the hills of the Black
Forest. Hiding from impending doom. Fog, snow, hail, the villages all dug themselves in more deeply than ever. The bombers
flew over, high overhead, maybe on their way to Berlin, on their
way to her friends, if they were still alive.

Emma rarely went outside, the Ruperts were not entirely certain that no one would give her away, the wife of a traitor. Months of isolation, they passed mechanically, mutely.

Judith was still asleep. The sleep of the innocent, the dreams of an exhausted nurse who would soon wake up startled to find the bed beside her empty, and the night over. Not yet, Judith, wait just a little longer.

She kept returning to the Black Forest that night. It had been the vacuum of her life, the interval, Carl dead, Bruno nowhere as yet, and Emma hidden away in the Black Forest. The symbolism of the name and place were not lost on her.

Helmut Wachter, whatever became of him? The Americans had taken him early one morning. What on earth did they want with a veterinary surgeon? From her room at the top of the house, Emma had seen them leading him away. She had knocked on her window, waved at him. He had waved back, calm, serious, almost polite, and without fear. She had found out later that they needed him as an interpreter, he knew some English. Since Christmas Eve, Emma had briefly spoken to him a few times. The story he had told that night in the church—none of Louis' stories was a match for it, no tales, or parables, or sermons.

If only it were true, that story, if you could truly dare to believe it at the end of your life. She had never forgotten Wachter's words, they fluttered in and out of Emma's head until the very end.

Hesitantly he begins, the veterinary surgeon among the church-goers, farmers, soldiers on leave or no longer able to fight, women without men, grandmothers, old men still hoping for a miracle, a few sleeping children. Vet and stand-in pastor, he is not a natural speaker.

"A man was walking along the beach, but it could have been a woman, I'm not quite sure. A person. Thinking about his life, maybe he didn't have much time left to live. He walked and he thought and, after a while, he turned his head and saw two sets of footprints in the sand—God was walking beside him. But whenever he remembered bad times, and times when he had been sad and despairing, he saw just one set of footprints.

"'Why weren't you there when I needed you most?' he asked God. And God replied that he had been walking with him all along. 'But why not in my times of greatest misery, when I missed you and needed you so much?'

"'Those were the days when I carried you.'"

And so the farmer and the mother and the soldier and the postman and the nurse and the schoolteacher and the woman in hiding were all united by a vet, thought Emma. How long it was before peace finally came.

28

After the light came the first sounds. Across the road, the grocer rolled up the iron shutters of his shop, the rattling of a new day. Seven o'clock, it was about to begin. The machinery was in motion, the members of the team were getting dressed, the pilot at the airport in Hamburg was checking his cockpit, Little Lenie, her cleaning lady, was dreading the morning when she would have to iron her employer's nightgown, her attire for the long night.

"Mrs. Verweij, what are you doing?!" Judith just about tumbled into the room, pale with shock.

"Nothing much, nurse, I didn't want to wake you, and I walked through here, there was no one around to carry me, as far as I could see."

Emma smiled, still half in the Black Forest, in Helmut Wachter's cold, damp church.

"I'll take you back, I'll get the wheelchair. You just stay there."

The angel, the caring soul. So young and so concerned about an old woman, a woman who dreamed and wandered and issued oracles in the form of proverbs and poems. Emma thought of the synonyms for her condition, they came to her easily, she was not mad, never had been, tired though, unspeakably exhausted.

The nurse expertly steered her back to bed. She arranged two pillows behind her back and put up the rails around the bed. Ready to set sail, and the pale pink blankets almost created the impression that it was pleasant. Judith would not move from her side now, that much was clear.

"What time is it, nurse?"

"Almost eight o'clock."

The clock as the final thing to hold on to at a moment when time was nearly out of sight. Everything was intertwined, past and present had become interchangeable. Sometimes Emma even had the feeling that she was beginning to overlap and coincide with the people she had lived with and loved.

She thought about Maria.

Maria Steinz, friend, neighbor, actress—admittedly manquée, but even so. Her laughter echoed over the balconies, worried neighbors looked up, pigeons fled the roof.

"Maria, quiet! The children are asleep," people shouted.

Which only increased the laughter. There was something exotic about her, she did not belong in the Low Countries, was impulsive and curious, and warm and welcoming. Maria conquered everyone she met. As she had Bruno. And Emma and so many others. Michael and Thomas too. The whole Verweij family had marched with her band. Year in, year out, carried along by her music. Viva Maria! How long had she been dead now? Emma tried to put the years in order, like the hours. It was almost impossible.

She was on a big, dark chessboard, being pushed back and forth, up and down.

She saw a tower, the tower of Loevestein, the magic word for boundless happiness, she thought of the little beaches along the Waal, where they swam in the summer.

They take the ferry from Vuren to Brakel. Sunlight flashes on the river, the ferryman steers clear of the heavily laden barges on their way to Germany. Bruno, hat on, hands in his pockets, spots the towers of the castle, far in the distance. Points at them, beckons Emma to get out of the car and to come and look. There! Look, there! With a grating sound, the ferry's ramp slides onto the shore, the cars cautiously make their way onto dry land, the captain on the bridge waves at everyone to hurry, he has to go back, there are cars already waiting on the opposite bank.

It was the summer of '56, Emma could not have been mistaken about that year. Whenever she thought about a summer, it was the summer of '56, the benchmark of her existence, compelling and vast in the smallest possible way, immovably fixed.

Bruno's skin complaint had broken out in full force, but in the summer the misery sometimes eased for a few weeks, the skin recovered and the growths, left and right, retreated. That summer, too. The summer when the first gaps in the street had appeared, the first houses were abandoned. The judge, the lawyer, the businessman, they had outgrown the war, they had discovered prosperity.

Maria and Maarten had moved to a place that Bruno and Emma had vaguely heard of but, once they had visited, no number of wild horses could have dragged them back.

"Helmond, it's all in the name," Maria always said. Maarten had become a director of a textile factory in this "hellmouth," where they manufactured fabrics worn by half the women in

Africa. And by Maria herself, who wore dresses with crazy patterns, as if someone had thrown the dressing-up box wide open. But she wore them with style, a white African, laughing, always laughing.

The Waal at Gorkum. Bruno's first memories are there—his father was the town's mayor before he was "promoted" to Gouda. Anyone who grows up along a river will always want to travel—could that be it? Not especially so for Bruno, although he often has to go abroad for his job. For him, it is more that anyone who has been a child beside a river will always long to go back. The wanderer returned. There! Look, there!

Emma gets out of the car and goes to stand beside him. She puts her hand into his inside coat pocket.

"I who hoist the white sails, sit at the helm and sing, life is a strange journey, our heart a gloomy thing."

Judith listened to the lines, which seemed to come from another world. She looked at Emma, whose eyes were closed. The words sounded as if she were speaking to someone.

My goodness, those words, another of her poets for sure, the woman was overflowing with old lines, once read and saved for the right moment.

Where was she now, Mrs. Verweij? Judith rested her hand on the bed rail.

"What if we bought a little house somewhere around here, wouldn't that be nice? I think we could manage it, it doesn't have to be expensive, and we could go at the weekends, it's three-quarters of an hour's drive."

Bruno is leaning over the rail of the *Brakel*. The waves of a passing boat slap against the side of the ferry, which gently sways. He takes Emma's hand out of his pocket and holds it to his cheek. Back to the river of his childhood, to the dyke villages and the water meadows that are flooded every winter.

Back.

Is Bruno's longing for the time before his sickness, for the war, for the street when it was still intact? For his father and mother? Emma wonders about this as they climb back into the car.

They drive along the Waal in their Renault 4CV, following the signs for Poederoijen and Woudrichem, heading into Munnikenland. Along the dyke, where goats are grazing and houses peep over, Bruno steers toward Loevestein, the castle he had seen as a child from the quay in Gorkum. A gloomy thing.

"Was your father in charge of Loevestein too, is it part of Gorkum?"

"He was in charge of everything his one eye could see."

Emma smiles, she has remembered the few stories that Bruno has told her about his father.

As an officer in the Royal Netherlands East Indies Army he had lost one of his eyes in a rebel attack in Aceh. Bruno was the youngest of the children, and the quietest. He was as gentle as his brother Rob was wild, and he did not cope well with arguments. The rift between Rob and their father had broken *his* heart, and their mother's, most of all, Emma had sometimes thought. The one-eyed officer barely reacted when his son Rob emigrated to South Africa, but Bruno had often wondered if that was not what had killed his father. Sadness that had turned inward and had no way out.

"It wasn't Staal who caused it, Emma. It was Rob."

He had lived in Gorkum until he was twelve, with his brothers, who had taught him to skate, swim and sail. They took him with them into the polders, and sometimes fought in town with boys from other neighborhoods, but he never wanted to join in with that. He preferred to go out skating, in the Bommelerwaard or the Alblasserwaard. As soon as the water froze, they were out on their skates. He later made the same trips with Michael and Thomas, unforgettable days on the ice.

He had not changed, Emma had often thought, but had remained a boy of twelve, who had never come all the way home, stopping halfway along the dyke to look out in amazement over the river and at the old landscape of his early years.

29

"Stop, Bruno, stop! There's your house!"

Beneath them is a potato field with a dyke house at its edge. The top floor looks out over the river in the distance and the silhouette of Loevestein beyond. On a post among the potatoes, barely visible, is a sign: FOR SALE. But the way it has been planted in the ground makes it seem more as if the house is not, in fact, for sale. A man dressed all in black and wearing a black cap is rooting around in the soil with a hoe. He would make a grave-digger look cheerful.

Once they are out of the car, they notice that the house is exactly at the point where two dykes meet, the Waaldijk and the Nieuwedijk.

"From Oudedijk to Nieuwedijk, the old to the new." They laugh, quietly, so as not to make the gravedigger uncomfortable.

"Excuse me. Is this house for sale?"

The man removes his cap, takes his pipe out of his mouth, thinks for a while, and then says, reluctantly: "It is."

In return, Bruno takes off his hat. He takes hold of Emma's hand and asks if they can come down there. They can. The steep stone steps to the house are overgrown with dandelions and grass.

"Versteeg," is all he says. His name. And then, after another lengthy pause: "So you'll be from the west, then?"

The thaw begins, Bruno is at his best. They drive back to Rotterdam, euphoric. Their street suddenly seems so small, without those floodplains outside the window.

"Call Maria," Bruno says, "the four of us are going to buy it together."

We're in. Sight unseen, comes the reply.

It is the beginning of a rural idyll, one that lasts almost a decade. For Emma, the house in the crook of the dyke becomes her most prized possession, from the summer of that year, 1956, Carl retreats into a safe shadow, and she can occasionally even think of him without that intense pain.

A patch of land at the foot of the dyke, large bushes of gooseberries, elderberries, reeds and roses, two pear trees and a shed, the vast empire of four city dwellers.

Helmond meets Rotterdam, is the motto. Maria and Maarten from the south, Emma and Bruno from the big city. "East, west—Brakel's best," Maria has had these words painted on a ceramic plate. Brakel is the name of the village that they are an offshoot of, theirs is the last house before kilometers of uninhabited land. Beyond is Munnikenland, which sometimes floods, and where nature dictates the rules.

Versteeg, the eel fisher, becomes their friend. As evening approaches and they put out their table and chairs on the Nieuwedijk, cars are a rarity there, he usually appears just in time for a glass of old jenever.

"Wouldn't say no."

"Cheers, Versteeg!"

"Here's to eternity, my friends."

Years later, Bruno helps to carry him through the village. In his coffin on their shoulders, through the streets of his life. Versteeg, who had twelve children, all of them born in that house on the dyke.

Emma opened her eyes, and quickly closed them again when she saw Judith's hand. She listened to the children going to school. Eight thirty, math or French, a class full of anticipation, reluctance and fun, the usual mutiny against incomprehensible teachers and stupid tests. All those classrooms full of children on a sunny morning, sunk in restless silence as the work lands on their desks—and then Emma in her bed, between heaven and earth.

Emma's thoughts drift effortlessly across the canal to the classes twenty meters away. And to Michael and Thomas' school years, the boys she had worried about all their lives, no matter how old they were.

Michael is acting. She is sitting in the auditorium of the Palace Theater, Bruno is not there, much to his regret. Ill at home. Michael has the leading role in a play by an English writer, scenes from the life of a dandy, they would settle for nothing less at that school. Slim and superior, he treads the boards at this ramshackle little theater, his acting transporting everyone to a London suburb in the 1950s.

Just before the interval he is sitting in a barber's chair, with his legs jacked up by the barber, who is waving his scissors like a beak, pecking at his head and cheeks. And as the barber delivers his lines, he cheerfully nips Michael's ear. A slow trickle of blood runs down his neck. From her place in the audience, in that bright illumination, it looks like a nasty wound. Is it real or is it a trick, berry juice artfully concealed in the barber's hand? But Emma, in one of the front rows, sees that it is not berry juice and finds it hard not to leap to her feet.

"Keep going," she hears him whisper to the barber. And they finish the scene, Michael and his torturer. The audience claps for minutes.

When Michael comes back on after the interval, a dark sticking plaster is poking up from beneath his roll-neck jumper, and before he can say anything, there is more applause. He looks at the spot where he thinks his mother is sitting, but she does not look back, as she is no longer there. Bruno cannot be left on his own for too long.

In truth, she has fled, at the sight of the neck and the blood in the neon light, and the sudden thought of Carl in the prison at Plötzensee. No blindfold, a camera was running and recording everything. A butcher's hook, an ice-cold industrial building, his neck, his throat.

Michael's star performance was soon followed by that other dramatic scene, the one in which she had lashed out at him in her fury. Emma's pointless act of revenge for his mean and childish comment about Carl.

But Thomas, who had also seen his elder brother performing that evening, had been left with a lifelong sense of admiration for him, he had told Emma. As the years went by, his imagination had turned it into an increasingly perilous evening, blood dripping onto the stage, his fellow actor panicking, and his brother sitting up high in his chair, the unruffled hero who did not abandon his role for one moment. The way something grows, becomes giant, grotesque.

30

Thomas would be taking off any minute, it was an hour's flight, she calculated for the umpteenth time. The countdown had begun. She found Thomas hard to fathom, but strangely that did not bother her, she had loved him and let him go his own way. She did not even feel the need to get any closer, she was not sure why. They knew each other inside out, he knew her better than perhaps anyone.

Emma had placed her ultimate fate in his hands, with complete confidence and with eternity already in her bones. The night was over at last, the day had been set in motion.

Emma in her bedroom, at first sight it looked like a still life, everything in order from A to Z, not one object too many, the curtains closed, the door to the balcony on its hook. Bruno's portrait, the pile of books, the dark mirror.

Jerusalem. A few years after Bruno's death, Thomas had asked her to go with him to the country her pastor had always talked about.

They arrive late in the evening, the *sherut* taxi takes the travelers to their addresses, one by one. Among them is a man with a beard, a skullcap and ringlets, and a long black coat. They stop for him in Mea Shearim, the neighborhood of the heavy-weights, the orthodox Jews. It feels like landing in another century. Out on the streets they can see fires surrounded by shadows, dark figures with books under their arms, swaying, half singing, an opera without women, which they watch and listen to from their taxi, with respect and incomprehension.

They are relieved to arrive at the American Colony Hotel in East Jerusalem, close to the Damascus Gate to the Old City. A hotel out of a book, their book.

Like lovers, they walk together through the tragic city built from ancient myths, lies and revelations. Wherever you look, you see an armed dream, a vision firmly fenced in.

Within the walls of the American Colony, East and West have found a kind of balance. Arab architecture and Irish whis-key. Flowers climb high over the four walls of the courtyard. At its center, lemon trees stand around a small pool, it smells like a forest. There are a few tables, with linen tablecloths, and Emma and Thomas sit there for hours in the evening, talking.

Or rather, Emma talks. She talks as never before, as though she has only just met the man in front of her and needs to tell him all about her life, urgently and completely. Her confession.

Until now she has only ever given Thomas a few vague hints, annoying puzzle pieces, scraps of conversations, but Emma's history suddenly makes an appearance, there, in the hotel courtyard, an unstoppable flow of stories, enough food for thought to fill him for decades, as Thomas later told her.

Bricks for a family cathedral, or a bunker, or a ruin. A little bit of everything. Her confession is a self-examination. There is so much that she has seen and not understood, she has fled her constantly repeating past for so long, she has been so afraid of the unknowable nature of everything, of the journey back. Now Emma is finally looking over her shoulder.

Berlin and the Black Forest are the hardest things to talk about. Yet that is what Thomas really wants to know. And about his father and his grandparents, mainly about his father, of course. But she notices how he keeps looking for an opportunity to come back to his mother's bricked-up past, the time before Bruno and the fury that exploded from it on that one unfortunate occasion.

Now and then the call from a minaret booms out, Allah must not be forgotten, prayers at the command of a hoarse metallic voice. Metal voices from loudspeakers, she knows all about that, Berlin had been infested with them.

And she tells her story, that old anger flaring up. She sees that Thomas is wondering whether to stop her, whether he really wants to know all of this, it is not what he intended, his curiosity has its limits. But she pulls him along with her, over that boundary, into the abyss of Germany, the filthiest years of the century.

No one has dared to speak Carl's name since Emma's fight with Michael. That name had become the black hole in their house, Emma was obviously aware of that, too. Now she says his name, naturally, as if she had not always kept it hidden away.

The slow encirclement, the growing isolation, the increasingly silent family, the loss of old friendships, her mother's unspoken disapproval, her father's concern: her life in Berlin had gradually become an exercise in loneliness. Carl's love was all that kept her going.

"How could you love a German, Mother?" he asks in an apologetic tone.

"It was impossible not to love him."

How do you explain why you fall in love with someone? How do you come up with an answer to such a simple but pointless question?

Yes, that was what it had been, impossible. She had not hesitated for a moment, almost from the first time she had met him she had wanted to protect Carl, to embrace him, to hold him tight. So very timid as he had asked if they would see each other again, and yet focused entirely on her, willing her to say yes. And she had answered without even having to think: "Yes, please. How about tomorrow?"

As she talks about her love for Carl, her pent-up rage is almost palpable. But she does not say everything, she holds something back, and Thomas can sense it.

"So when did he disappear, your Carl?"

A question his brother Michael could not have asked. Emma falls silent, time is getting on. A group of late guests drifts through the garden, pointing out the stars and the bright white moon. Suddenly there is the scent of jasmine, the scent of Berlin-Dahlem, of panic, a truck full of corpses being driven away down a road lined with bushes.

Her son, the doubting one, sits opposite her. With a question like a knife. Not again, Thomas, not back into the tunnel, with my heart that never became warm again. Nothing has disappeared, who and what was there has remained, been covered up, tenderly buried, rendered harmless, camouflaged until further notice. Carl became Bruno and Bruno became Carl, and my body forgot how and where. The arms around me—whose were they?

Emma does not reply, asks no question in return, she has become as quiet as the night above the hotel, her dress is sticking to her skin—she does not know if it is delayed grief or unexpressed anger, or just the heat in the courtyard. Watch with me for just one hour.

One of the guests approaches their table.

"Do you know, I met Lawrence of Arabia on this very spot,"—a small, rotund man with a thick American accent watches triumphantly as his remark cuts through their silence. Thomas does not react, Emma smiles.

"Peter O'Toole, or the real one?"

At that moment she remembers going to the cinema with Bruno and thinking that the man who played Lawrence was rather attractive. Bruno had been annoyed.

"The real one, of course."

The little man slinks off at this lack of respect. But his interruption was welcome.

"We'll go to the Old City tomorrow, and walk the Via Dolorosa. The real one."

Emma at her sharpest.

Their rooms open onto the courtyard, ivy around the doors, jasmine and wild geranium up the walls. It smells like her garden in Dahlem, her house in Brakel, like the Black Forest in late summer. Emma is sixty-nine years old, she still has years to go. At the door of her room she turns around and sees Thomas standing there, his room key in his hand. He gives her a wave, and then walks slowly on.

Since Bruno has been gone, Carl has been far away too, thinks Emma. No one disappears though, Thomas, but if only that were true.

31

The curtain in front of the balcony door moved, spring had begun in the street. The trees on the grass outside the house were blossoming pinkish red, cow parsley lined the banks of the canal, the first sailing boats were out on the lake. Just another Tuesday. A day to be born.

"Is there someone on the balcony, Judith? I thought I saw the curtain twitch."

"No, Mrs. Verweij, it's just the wind, there's no one out there."

"We always used to sit there, nurse. There's a ladder you can climb, through the hatch, onto the roof, it's so high that you can see the Waal, and Gouda. And, if you know where to look, the Black Forest."

Was this rambling, one of the signs of approaching death? Or lines of poetry? All Judith could do was straighten the blankets a little. They were Emma's first words since waking, a prophetess on the third floor, the lucid director of her final act. Caught between hunger and memory. But it was not actually hunger. A week of fasting banished the hunger in fact, the mind took charge of the body, Emma had become a sound chamber for her past. Everything tumbled over everything else, and if she could have sung, she would have.

"Was that the bell, nurse?"

"I don't think so, but I'll go and look."

It was the bell. Emma heard whispering in the hallway. It must be Little Lenie, who could iron so beautifully and who had helped her for years.

"Take care of Emma!" he had called, Bruno told her. She had been surprised and had not really understood why he had said that to Bruno. Three months after Rob's leaving party, a letter arrives from Cape Town with his death notice, along with details about the urn, an invoice for the cremation, and a statement of his assets—in the form of debts.

Shocked, Bruno read out the letter to Emma. Early evening, they are sitting on the balcony, the rain falling in sheets. It is not cold, and they do not want to be inside, this letter needs space.

Bruno answers her in a voice she does not know, so sad, when she asks why Rob actually left as a young man. His face is white, a sorry sight.

"It was to do with our father. It's a shame you never met him. We all looked up to him, admired him, but rarely showed him any affection."

The story of Rob and their father, who kept five or six spare glass eyes in the drawer of his bedside table. It had been March, Rob's birthday, his eighteenth. Their mother had laid the table for a party, Bruno and Rob were still at home, their older brother Hendrik was already studying. Rob spent more time out than at home too, a restless young man on a motorcycle, which he had earned and paid for himself, sometimes spending days riding across the Netherlands and Germany, with no reason or destination. A magical brother who was scared of no one. Not even their father.

The blow fell on the evening of his birthday, while the candles were burning and he was sitting on the chair that his mother had decorated with crepe paper. Out of nowhere, Rob accused his father of being a murderer in the jungle of Aceh.

"So how many Acehnese did you murder before they shot you down?" he had asked from his festooned chair.

Bruno could still hear the echo of his cold and heartless tone, as if Rob were not himself. Who was it who was saying such hurtful things, things that could not be unsaid—and why?

"Yes, I killed men who had just raped and strangled women and children. I wouldn't exactly call that murder. Maybe you'll be in a situation one day where you have to shoot or be shot. But I suspect—and hope—that you won't be."

The helpless, toneless answer and the beginning of the withdrawal. The silence between Rob and his father had never been broken.

"Do you know exactly what your father did in Aceh?"

"He left for the Dutch East Indies as a young officer, I have no idea why. The same need for adventure as Rob, perhaps. I still have letters from him and a few diaries from that time. He was writing about a completely forgotten war, the fighting and killing was atrocious. I've thought about Rob's outburst so often. But there's no way of telling if he was right or wrong, we don't know enough about the facts."

But he knew a good deal, as Emma discovers later, when she finds piles of books about Aceh after Bruno's death, filled with Bruno's notes and question marks. The confusion of wars and skirmishes, the mass murder. Her century, the years of fear.

* * *

Emma had also begun to read Bruno's father's diaries, and had become lost in them. It was the era of her own parents, of an outdated colonial world on the verge of collapse.

Bruno's father had been shot straight through the eye by a giant of a Sumatran when he entered a village with a small squad. He had climbed the stairs of a hut, it was silent all around, the locals must have fled. Suddenly a monstrously huge figure had appeared in the doorway, shouting something at him in a language he did not understand and pulling out a gun—not a klewang—from behind his back, and promptly shooting him. End of his military career. Back on a stretcher across the jungle he had fought his way through in the previous year, hurrah for peace, hurrah for the Netherlands, hurrah for the queen.

He had written so vividly about his journey inland, still with both eyes intact, armed to the teeth, ready to fight and prepared for ambushes, booby traps and snakes, that Emma saw his life as it must have been: absolutely dedicated to the army, to his men, to the greater idea that Aceh belonged to the Netherlands, that it was a dark hole to which light must be brought. Tales of derring-do contained between the black covers of an officer's report. But what was he doing in that jungle, she wondered. Fighting strangers, on the orders of strangers. Aceh, they had no business being there.

Emma had spent days in those notebooks, which Bruno had left for her. Bruno, her husband, had also tried to restore some kind of unity, always in search of connection and harmony. Mission failed—Rob had left, and his father had never been the same again.

32

"It's Little Lenie, Mrs. Verweij, you were right. And Big Lenie's here too."

Emma waved for the Lenies to come in. The little one in tears, the big one silently regarding the woman who had employed them for thirty years, who wanted to see them one last time, to hold their hands, hand in hand in hand.

Every Tuesday and Thursday they had come to the street, on bicycles, by bus, later in cars. In the undiluted stillness of their employer's flat, a woman who had become a friend, almost a mother and a grandmother. This trinity of lives intertwined, the seasons of work repeated over and over in every square meter. The slow and steady circulation of polishing silver, altering curtains, ironing and waxing furniture. The cupboards, the crockery, the paintings, the desk, the candlesticks, the beds—all according to an established cycle of dusting and replacing and changing. Spring cleaning, weekly cleaning, following the rhythm of nature, a holy order of things, a state of unshakable and irrevocable happiness.

No snake, no tree of knowledge, no fruit to pick in this house, which by the end of the day gleamed like a polished apple. Amen.

On the endless plains of their days together, which stretched out so far and for so long that memory no longer had any hold on them. Their voices had become so wholly familiar, as had the moment their key turned in the lock, the tap turned in the kitchen, the scent of coffee filled the flat, their work began.

She told the Lenies how grateful she was for all their work and asked if she could give them something. Big Lenie nodded and Emma pointed at a box beside the pile of books. There was an envelope of money for them too, but Thomas would find that later.

"My grandmother always used to wear these two rings, in the old days, when I lived with her in Leeuwarden."

As she spoke those words, she could picture the house on Eewal, the cobbled street with no traffic, and hear the maid humming as she polished the brass doorbell.

"They're for you. Or at least they are if you like them. Maybe you'd wear them every now and then and think of us, of my grandmother and me."

They laid their hands over and over on top of one another.

Leeuwarden in the 1920s, the roaring twenties, ha, even in the north the sun sometimes broke through. Emma as a twelve-year-old, the daughter of a diplomat, who had lived in Dublin and Brussels and Rio de Janeiro, suddenly among the farmers' sons and daughters at a strict school. Dream and trauma all in one. Caught between her grandparents' warmth and the loss of a free life in foreign cities. Watse lived there, the boy she grew up with, who had remained her only friend, even after she left for Germany.

The images slipped unnoticed into Emma's bedroom, just as quietly as the Lenies had left the room, it was over before she knew it. The bell chimed, nine thirty, ten o'clock, but no, the bells of the Koninginnekerk no longer existed, you had to rely on electricity for the time, on ugly dials, on the radio.

"The Führer miraculously survived an attempt on his life this morning, a sign that Providence protects the man who is destined to lead our people."

The radio predicts widespread raids throughout the country, the eradication of the enemy, the vermin will be chased from their holes, the cowardly attackers will not be safe anywhere. Their families will be arrested, their houses destroyed, they will curse the day they were born.

Carl, Adam, run!

Emma stared at the clock radio on her bedside table, a ray of sunshine fell across her bed, Judith had pulled back the curtain a little. Who had turned on the radio? Where was that menacing voice coming from? She could no longer trust her senses—was she dreaming it all? Everything seemed so utterly lifeless and there was a rushing inside her head, as if she were walking toward a sea, toward the surf. Which maybe she was, the sea no longer far away, the surf only a few more hours to go.

"Judith!"

"Yes, Mrs. Verweij. I'm here."

"Did you turn on the radio?"

"No, no, it's not on, would you like to listen to a little music, shall I look for something?"

Music! The portable gramophone with the Bakelite Marlene Dietrich records, with scratches in her voice and everyone on a dance floor the size of a newspaper. Not too loud, a party member lives across the road. Emma dances with Carl and with Adam as if her life depends on it. And that is how it is—dancing today, dead tomorrow. The bombers do not ask about age or political persuasion.

Thus far, their part of town has been spared and the British have generally flown to the center, but when would they discover Dahlem and Grunewald, the suburbs with the highest concentration of prominent murderers?

Her head against Carl's in a cradle of being lost and longing, they dance like children with no past and no thoughts of tomorrow. Adam and Clarita bump into them, laughing.

"Put on another record, Carl!"

33

The fragmentation was increasing. Emma lay looking at the scenes that were taking place just beyond her reach and detaching themselves from her bed. She had to hold off the demons for just a little longer, they were now pressing in on all sides. It had gone well so far, everything was following a mysterious but plausible plan. But it was at risk of derailing, her body was shattered, her brain almost in pieces.

Just a little longer, another half a day. First Michael, soon, then Thomas, then the team, thank God.

Michael, her elder son, so suddenly far more ill than his father had ever been. Thanks to that gradual assassin, Parkinson's, which slowly but surely locked you in, walled you up for good. First an emptiness inside the head, a loss of orientation, no longer being able to find your keys, then the growing panic about trivialities in a life full of information leaflets, side effects, and a fixed rhythm of pills. Emma had found his condition hard to bear, and that had fueled her guilt about her attack on him, an offense she had never been able to put right.

*   *   *

"Michael?"

Suddenly he was standing by her bedside, with his slight stoop. That was how he stood these days, as though the storm might break out at any moment.

"Michael?"

He looked at her, did not answer immediately. Took a handkerchief from his pocket and dabbed his cheek with it.

"Hello, I've just come round to see you, to say hello."

Emma saw that his hair was long by his standards, and automatically told him to go to the barber's.

"And watch out for your ear, Michael." She smiled, and so did he.

"Thomas called yesterday to say he's coming to help you. My little brother the nurse. Sister Thomas."

So he knew. Michael had not visited much in the past few months. Emma had understood, he had enough difficulty with his own condition, with the delusions that were taking hold of him.

"Yes, he's going to help me, Michael—he said he'd be here at about eleven. The doctor's coming too."

Had he heard what she said? Where was he? His face had become unreadable, nothing moved in it, the cheeks of parchment, the eyes unnaturally dull and inward-looking. Michael was looking inward and no one knew what he could see.

"Bye, Michael. Bye, Mickey." She called him by his old nickname, from before the dawn of time, from before consciousness. He just stood there in his haze, as if he had stepped in by accident, or had forgotten why.

"I'll be off, then," he said.

He laid his hand on her head, on the thin white hair, an unintentional blessing—or maybe deliberate, who could say?

Emma put her hand over her eyes. It was so dark beneath her hand, so directionless.

She heard the click of the door as Michael closed it behind him, heard his footsteps and the tap of his walking stick. For a moment, she fell asleep, she needed strength to welcome the doctor with a clear head. She would probably start asking questions, one final check to find out if Emma knew what she was saying and what she wanted. A good woman, her doctor, but without a jot of humor.

34

"Shalom."

It could be only one person. Since their trip to Jerusalem, that had always been their greeting, slightly ironic, but always with the memory of that week in the white city, where the word "shalom" was on the optimistic side. But today it hit the mark.

She did not want to react to his voice yet, wanted to absorb the sound into herself, to take it with her, to keep it for later, for the hours alone.

What would he think of her short hair? A week before, she had decided that she had had enough of it. Just before she had stopped eating, she had asked Judith to take the scissors to her hair, the hair she had cherished for decades and had put up in a kind of wave, day after day. With a subtle maneuver, she had always folded her long hair into a timeless style. But for the past few months she had no longer been able to lift her hands behind her back and neck, so her hair hung loose, a symbol of surrender.

Thomas, her "German son," as she liked to call him. What on earth was he doing in Germany? He said he felt at home there, that he found Hamburg so much more expansive and welcoming than Holland. Few cities had been as devastated as

Hamburg, and rebuilt with such subtlety and style. Such a difference from Rotterdam.

Did Clarita still live there? Was she still alive? The corre-
spondence that had begun after their chance encounter had
eventually come to an end, everything had been said, every
word about their shared past and their husbands. They had
drawn a line under it before they started repeating their stories.

Emma would have to ask Thomas to find out where she was
now, and then he could meet her if he wanted to. Clarita and
Adam had two daughters, both born during the war. The courage of having children then, taking a stand against the flow of
history.

One afternoon in 1943, Clarita comes to see Emma, one child in
a pushchair, the other on the way. Disaster is in the air, signs of
breakdown all around, and Clarita is heavily pregnant, the very
image of confidence. But it is a sham, she is at her wits' end.

"He keeps traveling all over, but wherever he goes he hits a
brick wall, the Allies won't listen to him. He flew to Stockholm
yesterday, and he wants to go to Venice next, and who knows
where else. The Gestapo must be tracking his movements. Even
though he's said nothing, I'm sure he's involved in the conspir-
acy against Hitler."

"I know, Clarita. Carl is involved too. And he's trying to keep
up with Adam, but Carl says he's only becoming more restless
and worried. I think we just need to let them get on with it, even
though I'm as scared as you are."

Emma jumped when Thomas gently shook her shoulder.

"You're here, at last. How was the flight?"

A short delay, but he had been able to fly directly to Zestienhoven, it could not have been any faster. His father had given

his best years to that airport. Long meetings with influential types in Rotterdam, along with civil servants from The Hague and specialists in aviation law. It was the late 1950s, but the idea had taken hold of Bruno and his friends some time before, and everyone was busily working away. On a vision that actually became reality: an airport for Rotterdam, not much bigger than a bowling alley, but it was there.

Bruno on the way to the airport or back, on an icebreaker at the port, with a fishing rod by the water in Brakel, on his bicycle, in his hat, in long white trousers on the tennis court, pale as death in an endless series of hospitals. Bruno, with whom she had led a double life for so long, as perhaps he had with her. Love is not that easy to uproot and replant. From Berlin to Rotterdam. She had done it, and yet she had not.

Zestienhoven, had Thomas said Zestienhoven? It was the sound of the most tender of times, the street still in the familiar arrangement. Brakel found, no sign of the war. Emma at her most beautiful, Maria always cheerful, friendship around every corner and time passing slowly and infinitely.

It was then that she had once seen Bruno and Maria walking hand in hand, along the dyke by Loevestein.

There is nothing mysterious or forbidden about it, it is happy and light-hearted and with no ulterior motives, secrets or hidden passion. Maarten saw it too, Bruno and Maria, the children, everyone together on the beach by the Waal, near the castle. That is the way it was, so innocent and isolated.

Walking along a dyke, a picture cut out of a book, the fairy-tale castle in the background, children swimming in the river, meadows all around, on the water a boat with a woman at the helm, a flock of starlings high in the sky, cows with their hoofs in the water, a brick factory in the distance sounding the signal for lunch.

Emma saw it and never forgot. That was how to walk and to live and to love and to outwit death. That was how Carl and she had once walked on the shores of the Wannsee on Sunday mornings, or along the streets of Grunewald, free and with no history.

The vision passed before Emma's downcast eyes. Thomas waited for her to speak.

Zestienhoven, where she had dropped Bruno off so many times, when he urgently needed to go to Germany with K.P. again, always to that dreaded Germany, which haunted her sleep. Where they murdered Carl—she does not even know where his grave is, he has no grave. Never looked for it, never thought of going to look for it. Dumped probably, burned and scattered, plowed in, carried on the wind. Enemies of the state.

Emma sensed Thomas looking at her—and how much good it did her.

"You have to find Carl's grave, Thomas. Do you think it's possible, did they keep a record, they must have done, they kept a record of everyone and everything."

What a task. Thomas promised without hesitation, he would track it down, absolutely, he would take care of it.

He lowered the fence around the bed and sat on the edge, close, almost touching her. Emma rested her hand on his arm, as if they were about to go for a walk. His journey still all around him, not even his scarf removed, summer coat on, ready to leave, that was how Thomas sat there.

"That time in Jerusalem, I've often thought back to that evening in the courtyard of the American Colony Hotel—I'm so sorry for burdening you with far, far too many intimate details. Do you remember the look of dismay on that American's face, though, the man who was so proud of his Lawrence of Arabia?"

Thomas laughed, as if there were nothing in the air, nothing about to happen. His mother seemed able to recall her life in flashes and fragments, without worrying about time or sequence. In exquisite detail, almost like a play, as a carefree observer.

"Yes, he was so deeply offended that he went striding off. We saw him in the Garden of Gethsemane later, too—do you remember? And we heard him declaring to someone in his party that he'd met Lawrence at exactly that spot. The Judas. We were crying with laughter when we left the holy site, and you said it was most inappropriate."

Emma looked at Thomas. The way he spoke, it lifted her up. Her life had gradually come to a standstill, but when he was around it momentarily sprang back into motion. Thomas, who had painlessly slipped away from her, who was so close to her, even though he lived abroad and was always traveling.

"New hairdo, Mother? Very perky."

The seriousness was yet to come, although Emma's request had been weighty enough. But they never managed to go for long without a few little jokes. He was the only one who could still make her laugh.

"I couldn't put it up anymore. It's so strange, that your own arms can become too heavy to lift. My hair was just hanging there, doing nothing. So Judith cut it off for me. They say hair has no sense of feeling, but it hurt all the same."

A joke? Honesty? What she said sounded so ordinary, so beyond any suspicion of pretension. Hair that hurts, strength ebbing away. What had for so long been part of an animated life—take out the scissors, chop it all off.

Tuesday morning, April 29, 2008. Thomas saw his mother's diary lying open, one of those big art diaries from Museum Boijmans, in which she had noted her daily business for as long as anyone could remember. In her distinctive handwriting. "My scrawl," she called it. A hand at war with the language. Right to the last she had written with letters that grew bigger and bigger, as if she were constructing a defensive wall.

Emma's gaze followed his, she pointed at the diary, asked him to keep all her letters and papers and take them to Hamburg. She had prepared for this moment, rehearsing what she wanted to say. This was her legacy, she had nothing but some old pieces of paper, the flotsam of history.

"Letters from Clarita von Trott, and from Bruno, and from Rob. And from Mr. Wapenaar, whom you sadly never knew. He slipped away quietly, his letters are about his friendship with your grandfather. Don't throw them away, Thomas, don't throw anything away. Oscar's letters from the days I was at school in Leeuwarden and lived with my dear grandparents, I kept them because . . ." Emma hesitated. "I kept them because they were the nicest letters I ever received from him. Every word is full of longing for the time we were still together, in Rio and Dublin and Brussels. They'd left me behind in the Netherlands and were roaming the world, but you know that already. And still, if there's one place I felt at home, it was in Leeuwarden. With Watse . . ."

Emma paused. What she had said was still hanging in the air. Thomas saw how tired she was and how much effort it took for her to continue.

Skating with Watse, her childhood friend from Leeuwarden, her protector, the man who had warned her so often about Naziland, where no one was any good and no love could ever last. Skating across the Frisian lakes, black ice, she could hear the blades swishing, a sound that echoed across eighty years.

They put on their wooden speed skates and fall into a swift rhythm, racing toward a horizon of wild geese, snowy skies, sunrises and sunsets. Without tiring, they skate along after each other, into their youth and an unknown future.

A bullet in the back for Watse. But no, it was not a bullet. Much later she hears that he was not shot while trying to escape at all, as she was told at first. He had fled the Netherlands, and went to Sweden and then the East Indies, where he died.

It was a false rumor, and she had cried for him in Berlin, while he was still alive. She had mourned as he was sailing on a boat to Stockholm, she had pictured him falling down dead, she was exhausted with grief for him.

Then, then, in that terrible city, in that sinister building on Prinz-Albrecht-Strasse, the Gestapo headquarters, where she is humiliated and interrogated by a lewd and leering man who smokes and taps his shoe on the floor, that tapping on the bare concrete floor, that brazen, indifferent tapping. That leg, with its crude and nasty foot.

It is a miracle that she is released, still just under the protection of Adam von Trott from Foreign Affairs, Carl's boss and their friend.

She forced herself to leave that episode alone, the time she was taken in for questioning because she and Carl had gone to Geneva with Adam and had spoken to her father. She had been locked up for only a few hours, but that afternoon had taken years to shake off.

The letters, back to the letters, she could feel that she was slipping away. Back now, back to Thomas, he was waiting for her.

"Thomas?"

"Yes, Mother, I'm here, go on. You were talking about Grandfather and someone called Watse, I think, where did you suddenly disappear to? You stopped, you seemed a long way away."

"Berlin, I was in Berlin. Will you look up Adam and Clarita's daughters?"

It was all going too quickly for Thomas now, she was flying back and forth, her past was emerging from all over, and he could barely make sense of it. Daughters? Yes, yes, he would look them up, did she know them? No, only as a little girl and a baby.

She had rehearsed everything so thoroughly, endlessly repeating it to herself on those evenings at her window. Where everything was that Thomas had to take with him, the ten boxes at the back of her wardrobe, her diaries, the drafts of the letters she had written, the locked desk drawers full of stories never told.

She had torn up the letters from Louis years ago and thrown them into the fire. Fire that blazed, like the words themselves. He had worshipped her, as only a believer can.

Thomas would not have to read them, he would not have understood. Who would? Who understands his own life? Who hears the song of another's heart? Nothing lasts, nothing catches fire that was not born of fire. Out of how much ash is a bird reborn?

Where did those lines come from, her head was glowing, her bed had narrowed to a furnace of ancient poems and thoughts.

"Hold my hand if you like."

Thomas, the nurse.

"Take care of Michael, Thomas."

Echo, echoes. Doubled sounds, too many, piercing music. She had lived for this morning with her son. Now that he was finally here, it was all happening so quickly. The dykes were breaking, her tough resistance and the last remnants of control were melting away.

"He's so terribly alone. So lost, and I haven't been able to help him. I sent him to the barber's, his hair was rather long. Do you remember, Thomas, that barber and the blood running down his neck?"

"Yes, Mother, I remember everything, I'll take care of him, I'm his brother."

"There's a letter from a woman called Lara van Oosten. But don't read it, just throw it away. I didn't tear it up, as it was written with such great love for my father. Long story, too long for now, rubbish bin. Do you hear me, Thomas?"

Lara's letter had been written not long after their meeting in the mountains, Emma had chanced upon it again just after she had resolved to stop eating. In the giddiness of those first days without food, she had found Oscar once more, and remembered the conversation with Lara, the morning after they first spoke in the lobby.

* * *

It is brilliant weather, the mist has lifted, the mountains look freshly washed. It is so warm, in fact, that they can have breakfast outside. Lara's husband has taken the little train into the village and left them together on the terrace, like the discreet diplomat he is. An early November day that feels like summer, with soft light on the Jungfrau, the kind of day when everything is self-evident, transparent, free.

Lara is talking, she is speaking about Oscar so very differently than the evening before, when her husband had been watching from a distance and, almost feverishly, at full speed, she had made a sort of confession. But now, the next morning, in this state of weightlessness, her months with Oscar are coming to life and she sketches dream-like days with him.

Emma has rarely heard anyone talk about love like this, so unselfishly, so naturally. Bern in May in the war years, in the depths of that criminal era, alongside tourists who deny everything, and soldiers who maintain a semblance of readiness. Their days together, their lives slowing down. The turmoil over, time seems to dissolve, every question has become redundant, and so there are no more answers either.

"Love there seemed like death, so absolute and so still."

It was a sentence from Lara's letter.

Whose voice is speaking that morning? Lara's? Or Emma's?

Change Bern to Berlin and swap Oscar for Carl, and you have a similar story of an exceptional love. Startling and strange and enough to last a lifetime.

36

"Maria's letters."

"Yes, Mother."

"Don't go away . . ."

"I can't hear you. Speak up."

Had she nodded off, was she asleep? She heard Thomas from a distance, as if he were not sitting beside her but floating somewhere above her in space.

"Stay there, Thomas. Don't fly off again."

"You were talking about Maria's letters. Where are they?"

"They're all together, in labeled boxes at the back of my wardrobe. Go and take a look—I've bundled them together, you can't miss them."

Inheritor of old paper, gatherer of old histories, Thomas was supposed to make something of this kindling for the memory. His mother's chronicler, that was more or less what Emma had in mind, that was what she had repeated to herself so many times, rethought, revised.

Thomas returned from his journey through her wardrobe, she had heard the doors slide, and then the rummaging through her clothes. He said he had found the boxes and would take them with him.

Maria's letters. Reading letters was the only thing that still mattered, all that remained and would be left behind. Fence around a life, access to hidden secrets and cherished lies. God's ways may be mysterious, but Emma's paths had not been exactly straightforward either. That was how she saw it.

She lay there, red-rimmed eyes looking upward, away from Thomas, who had sat back down on her bed.

Maria, Maria Steinz, Maria Mandemaker as she was called as a girl. There was no name more suitable. A maker of baskets woven from dreams, to catch you, to rock you. The Pied Piper of Gorkum, where she grew up along the same river as Bruno, although they had never met each other there. She was a little older and mixed with a different crowd.

They did not meet until so many years later, in their street, in a time of war and enchantment. How they would get together, in those years of danger, after a raid, with beer and wine, and spend the night, filled with relief, in a tangle of past fear and emerging love. Their street, twenty buildings long, bordered by a canal and a school. They had all been healthy but poor, and filled with reckless optimism. That was how she had described it to Emma in the many letters that came from all over, wherever the wind or the train had taken her.

After Bruno and Maarten had died, she was forever on the move, increasingly reluctant to stay put. When she was not traveling, she began to think, and to worry, and soon felt cornered. Traveling ahead of her memories, like the bird that flees the storm and serves as a warning. Her motto: "I put my head in the sand to keep my head above water." Humor. She also liked to quote Chris Dudok, who said that it was impossible to

be too deaf in this world. It was not humor. He meant it. So did
Maria, in fact.

Should she perhaps ask Thomas to throw away Maria's letters? He would read about his father, how the two of them had
gone through the war together. He might suspect Maria had
meant much more and had been his lover for far longer, maybe
always. Was that the case? No, not always, Maria had sworn it
was not, only during the war. But yes, the war went on, it had
never stopped, not for anyone. Not for Maria, not for Emma,
not for Bruno, and not for Chris and Clarita, Oscar and Kate,
and Rob and Helmut Wachter.

God, Helmut Wachter, that sweet veterinary surgeon with
his story about the walker on the beach. Emma would like
to glance back for footsteps in the sand. But who would be
able to pick her up? She was as heavy as death—no God was
a match for that.

The bell rang in the hallway, twice. The appointment with
the doctor.

37

The sun was shining in on all sides, the windows reflecting the light. The school was about to empty, nothing at all to alarm anyone walking past, or cycling, or parking a car alongside the wide pavement in front of the building.

Half past three. Emma drowsed a little, now and then, the doctor's visit had tired her out. They had inserted a catheter, much against her will, but she had eventually allowed herself to be persuaded that it was necessary and that otherwise the sedation team would do it. The humiliation had already faded, there was only surrender to what was to come. Chosen for herself, prepared and managed down to the last detail.

The doctor had asked again if she consented to the next steps: sedation, unconsciousness and slow, painless death.

Painless? My dear doctor, my dear woman, what are you talking about? These hours *are* the pain, everything in me and around me is loss and abandonment. The world is contracting with old wounds and wasted time and regret. It has grown cold and bare, empty, completely still. Painless—if only. True enough, nothing is burning, no knife is stabbing, no nerve is twinging, no one is pulling at me with hooks, although physically the anesthesia may be perfect, I know your drugs will make sure of that.

Between waking and sleeping, Emma on her final journey back, talking to the doctor, who has left, waking and falling back to sleep, dreaming and waiting. The afternoon hours. She had told Thomas to go into the dining room until they came.

"You have to eat properly"—the mantra of her motherhood. Lenie had laid the table for lunch. She wanted to be alone for a little while.

Strange, to want to be alone now, it felt like the sea retreating before the tidal wave hits the shore, the language of the condemned. To be alone, and then to be no more.

Displaced, alienated, leaving home, the street, the countries where she had been, everything was empty, there was no railing, nothing to hold on to, endless space, no horizon in sight. Flat out, she lay between clean sheets, with a tube snaking across her lap to catch the last drops of liquid. The paraphernalia for the end.

"Why Canada, Bruno? I've no real objections. Of course I'll go with you, and the boys are young enough. But we don't know anyone there and how on earth are we going to run a farm? You're even less of a farmer than I am. And the others don't have a clue either, they're all fingers and thumbs."

In Emma's spirit realm, everything is piled up together, millions of words and conversations. The smallest things suddenly become large and vivid.

"But there are four families going, Maarten and Maria are the only ones who don't want to come."

Is he unwittingly running from Maria? By the winter of 1954, the street has almost lost its magic, the first dissidents have left their houses and gone out into the world. Bruno and three of the other men have come up with the idea of emigrating. A temporary confusion, a restricted focus, a dissatisfaction with the order they want to leave behind, rebels on a small scale, but equipped with the right connections and with ambitious plans.

Becoming a farmer in Canada, creating a small settlement for four families with room for more. They have read too many books, it would seem, too many rural idylls. It is a sorry attempt to break away from—yes, from what? From a life all planned out. Later they laugh about it and tap their foreheads. They must have been mad. Out of their minds. God, what were they thinking?

God, the three-letter word, which Louis bandied about and Emma borrowed from him for as long as she was able.

Where was He now, where were His footprints? Nothing moved.

"Lord God, we have become strangers by listening to Your voice." Louis is standing in a pulpit high above her in a dark church in the city center, one that happened to have been spared by the German bombers. Emma has indeed become, for a time, a very brief time, something of a stranger to herself by listening to Louis' voice, to his stories and poems, with its gigolo charm. It was he who had introduced her to Nijhoff and to Vroman and Rilke and all the others.

But she had never felt more of a stranger in the world than she did now. Or nearly home, awakened, back to the beginning, at the edge of the world. Whoever has no house now will never build one. Chris, Chris, you're not answering the phone, you're avoiding me, I was supposed to be coming to stay.

Was it Julia, or was she merely an excuse because he did not want to go on? She had been dead for forty years, you went into the depths with a big iron ball on your feet, you denied her, you thought you were faithful to her, but you betrayed her free spirit. You are my faint-hearted brother, my ally, your death touched no one more than me. Chris Dudok, where are you, I'm drowning here, my head is about to switch off like a lamp.

Emma opened her eyes, and felt how dry they were. The moisture had seeped away, as if there were no point to sadness now, as if tears were in the past.

She listened. To no one, there was no one, there was no sound that seemed familiar. But yes, there was, it seemed she could hear Thomas' voice through her bedroom door. Maybe he was on the telephone, or talking to Lenie. Or was the team already there?

Sun over Texel, with sheep as far as the eye could see. Their tent is just behind the dunes, Den Burg is within walking distance but there are no people around. It is early in September, and Bruno has asked Emma if she—he would not make a habit of it—would like to go camping with him on Texel, the island where he was born, where his father had his first post as mayor. He had played there for seven years, and the scent of the dunes and the sand had never left him. Maybe his farming fantasy, the idea of going to Canada, had something to do with it, a big child missing the wide open spaces and the sea and the surf. He shows Emma everything he still remembers, they cycle across the island and stand in front of the old mayor's house, where nothing has changed and every brick is familiar.

"There was a crowd of beachcombers in morning coats waiting for my father when he first arrived at the town hall. They'd heard that he was a retired officer and had been expecting an older man with a mustache and sideburns and a cigar in his mouth. Then a lad of twenty-eight stepped into the council chamber, with only one eye and a beautiful wife and two small children. Apparently his response was to say: 'At ease, men—and coats back in the cupboard.'"

Their tent with airbeds and a primus stove, everything for the first time, everything still wide open, no child on the way as yet.

She heard the bathroom door open, various unfamiliar footsteps, then the bedroom door. Thomas, a woman she did not know, a man she did not know, it was like a little procession.

She and Bruno walk at the back, the streetlights are on, windows are illuminated here and there in the dark rows of houses. Ahead of them, in a large group of children, they see Michael and Thomas, they are carrying lanterns on sticks. Carefully, they have to hold their candles upright, and keep their hands over the openings of the lanterns to protect them from the wind. One false move and the whole thing could go up in flames.

A procession of lights and children's eyes, Emma and Bruno following behind. The children's crusade moves on, with mothers and fathers dropping out along the way. At home, the candles burned out, the lanterns are folded up and put away for the following year.

Goodbye, queen. Goodbye, winter. May is nearly here.

* * *

"Mother, here are the people who have come to help you."

Quiet voices, children's feet, rustling, coats off, it is cold out. Stay up for a moment, boys, stand at the window and look out. They gaze into the night, at where they just walked with their flickering lanterns, dancers on their way to bed.

It is late, perhaps nine already, their eyes and legs are suddenly heavy with sleep. Emma picks them up, first one, then the other, carries them to their room and closes the curtains.

"Mother, Mother."

Very slowly Emma turned her head to the side. She struggled to remember where she was, to work out who the people were around her bed. Lined up to provide help, moral support. Motionless, alert and even friendly, to a degree. She tried to nod at them, to reassure them.

"Yes, Thomas. I can hear you, what is it?"

"Here are the people who have come to help you."

They said their names, politely and as if it mattered. Greeting and farewell in a name, in a brief nod of the head.

The team, bags in hands, velvet gestures and inaudible actions. Silently at work. Words were the enemy, silence their best camouflage. The only sound was the humming of the electric bed as they raised Emma's head a little higher. Tubes were rolled out, a device hung on the railing of the bed, the end could begin any minute now.

Emma watched as if it were nothing to do with her. And indeed it was nothing to do with her, she was not there, she was everywhere, but not there.

* * *

Escaped, far beyond the reach of any snaking tubes, on the lookout. Up the ladder, across the roof, to their chimney. Clouds fanned out, racing across the city. She has never been embraced like this, Bruno's mouth on hers, his hands cupping her face, the sensation that she will never come back down to earth, forever fugitive, nowhere to be found, moved on, freed from the old days.

Sounds of the street, seagulls, the school erupting, sailing boats on still water, the trees in full blossom in the depths. And would she like to stay, with him and in the street below.

She is awake, finally awake.

OTTO DE KAT is the pen name of Dutch publisher, poet, novelist and critic Jan Geurt Gaarlandt. His award-winning novels have been widely published throughout Europe. *The Longest Night* draws together elements from three previous novels published by MacLehose Press: *Man on the Move* (2009), *Julia* (2010) and *News from Berlin* (2014).

LAURA WATKINSON is a translator from Dutch, Italian and German whose translations include works by Cees Nooteboom, Jan van Mersbergen, Tonke Dragt and Peter Terrin.